KU-312-109

GREY SOULS

France, December 1917: Daily life continues in a small town near the Front, despite the pounding of artillery fire and the parade of wounded strangers passing through its streets. Then any lingering sense of normality is destroyed with the discovery of a strangled ten-year-old girl in the freezing canal. A deserter is convicted of her murder and executed, and the case closed. Years later, one man is still trying to make sense of these events, while struggling with the tragedies and demons of his own past. But excavating the town's secret history will bring neither peace nor justice . . .

Books by Philippe Claudel
Published by Ulverscroft:

MONSIEUR LINH AND HIS CHILD

PHILIPPE CLAUDEL

GREY SOULS

Translated from the French by Hoyt Rogers

Complete and Unabridged

ULVERSCROFT
Leicester

2017

First published in Great Britain in 2005 by
Weidenfeld & Nicolson

First Large Print Edition
published 2017
by arrangement with
MacLehose Press
An imprint of Quercus Publishing Ltd
An Hachette UK company
London

The moral right of the author has been asserted

This book is a work of fiction. Names, characters,
businesses, organisations, places and events are either
the product of the author's imagination or are used
fictitiously. Any resemblance to actual persons, living
or dead, events or locales is entirely coincidental.

Copyright © 2003 by Editions Stock
English translation copyright © 2005 by Hoyt Rogers
All rights reserved

A catalogue record for this book is available
from the British Library.

ISBN 978–1–4448–3405–5

Published by
F. A. Thorpe (Publishing)
Anstey, Leicestershire

Set by Words & Graphics Ltd.
Anstey, Leicestershire
Printed and bound in Great Britain by
T. J. International Ltd., Padstow, Cornwall

This book is printed on acid-free paper

1

It's very difficult to find the beginning. So much time has gone by that words will never bring back — and the faces too, the smiles, the wounds. Even so, I must try. I have to cut open the belly of the mystery and stick my hands deep inside, even if none of that will change a thing.

If somebody were to ask me how on earth I know all the things I'm going to recount, I'd answer that I just do. I know them because for twenty years they've been as familiar to me as the fall of night and the dawn of day. Because in fact I've spent my life trying to piece them together, to put them into place. So they can speak and I can listen. That used to be my job, more or less.

I'll be calling forth a lot of shadows, but one will be out front. It belongs to a certain Pierre-Ange Destinat. He was the prosecutor in V for more than thirty years, and he plied his trade like clockwork, never faltering, never breaking down. Actually, you could say he was an artist, and he didn't even need a museum to show his art. In 1917, at the time of the Case — as people here called it, always with a sigh it seemed — he was over sixty and had retired only the previous year. Though he hardly spoke, he always made a great impression. He was a tall, impassive man who resembled an indifferent bird, far-off and majestic, with pale eyes that never seemed to move and lips whose thinness he didn't bother to disguise with a moustache. His forehead was high and his hair a most distinguished grey.

V is about twenty kilometres from our town. Twenty kilometres in 1917 was very far indeed, especially in winter — especially in a war that showed no interest in ending. The war caused great commotion on the roads as they became jammed with handcarts and trucks, flooded with stinking fumes and thousands of thunderclaps. Even though the front was fairly near, from our town it seemed an invisible monster, another country.

Destinat was known by different names, depending on whom one asked and where. Among the inmates in the jail at V, he was generally called Bloodsucker. In one cell I even saw a drawing of him, carved with a knife on the thick oak door — not a bad likeness in fact. Admittedly, the artist had had plenty of time to admire the model during the fifteen long days of his trial.

When we ran into Pierre-Ange Destinat on

the street, the rest of us called him Mr Prosecutor. Men raised their caps to him, and women of the humbler sort curtsied. Fine ladies of his own social class would incline their heads ever so slightly, like little birds when they drink from gutters. Whatever the greeter or greeting, it seemed no matter. He didn't answer — or did it so faintly you would have needed highly polished double-strength spectacles to see his lips move. But it wasn't disdain, as most believed; I think it was simply detachment.

All the same, there was one young lady who had almost understood him, a girl I will speak of again and who called him Sadness, a nickname she kept to herself. Maybe it's her fault that everything happened, but then she never knew anything about it.

At the beginning of the century, a prosecutor was still a figure of great importance. And in time of war, when a single hail of bullets could mow down a whole company of solid lads, seeking the death of one lone man in chains required craftsmanship. I don't think he acted out of cruelty when he went after the head of some poor slob who had battered the postman or disembowelled his mother-in-law. The thug would stand in handcuffs before him, between two officers, but at best Destinat hardly noticed him. He looked right through him, as he if had already ceased to exist. Destinat never prosecuted a flesh-and-blood criminal; he defended an idea, simply an idea: his own idea of good and evil.

When his sentence was pronounced the convicted criminal would howl, burst into tears, or fly into a rage. Sometimes he'd raise his hands to heaven, as if he'd suddenly remembered his catechism. By now, though, he was entirely invisible to Destinat. The prosecutor would be putting his notes away in his briefcase, four or five sheets on which he'd composed his closing argument, purple ink in his small refined script, a handful of well-chosen words that reliably made the court shudder and the jurors reflect, unless they were asleep; a few words that were enough to erect a scaffold in double-quick time, faster and more surely than two journeyman carpenters could have done in a week.

He bore no grudge against the condemned. I saw the proof of that with my own eyes, in a hallway just following the verdict. Destinat emerged with his Cato-like air, his beautiful ermine still on his back, and came face-to-face with the Widow's future husband — the Widow, that's what they called the guillotine. The prisoner harangued him plaintively, eyes still red from having just heard his awful fate, and now full of remorse that he'd ever pumped those gunshots into his boss's gut. 'Mistah Prosecutor,' he whined, 'Mistah Prosecutor . . . ' Destinat looked him right in the eye, oblivious to the bailiff and the handcuffs, put a hand on his shoulder, and answered, 'Yes, my friend. We've already met, haven't we? What can I do for you?' As sincere as you please — no mockery at all. The condemned man looked stunned. It was as if a second sentence had been pronounced on top of the first.

Following the end of every trial, Destinat would have lunch at the Rébillon, across from the cathedral. The owner is a fat man with a pate white and yellow like a head of chicory and a mouthful of rotten teeth. His name is Bourrache. He's not very clever, but he has a good head for money. That's his nature: no fault of his. He always wears a large apron of blue wool that makes him look like a girthed-up barrel. He used to have a wife who never left her bed; she suffered from sluggishness, as we say in this region, where it's not uncommon for certain women to confuse the November fogs with their own distress. When she finally died it was less on account of this illness — which after a time she'd probably put on as a permanent mantle — than because of what had happened,

5

because of the Case.

At the time, the Bourrache daughters were like three little lilies, but with a pure touch of blood that brightened their complexions to a glow. The youngest was barely ten. She had no luck — or maybe she had a lot. Who knows?

The other two were known simply by their first names, Aline and Rose, while everyone called the smallest one Belle and a few would-be poets made it Belle-de-jour — Morning Glory. I used to see all three of them in the room, carrying carafes of water, litres of wine, and silverware, among dozens of men who talked too loudly and drank too much, and it seemed as if someone had arranged flowers to relieve the sordidness of the atmosphere. And even in the company of her sisters, the little one looked so unspoiled as to seem not of our world.

When Destinat entered the restaurant, Bourrache — a man of habit — always treated him to the exact same greeting: 'Another one cut down to size, Mr. Prosecutor!' Destinat would never answer, and Bourrache would show him to his seat. The prosecutor's table, one of the best, was reserved for him year-round. I didn't say the best, because that would have been the one nearest the enormous earthenware stove beside the window hung with crocheted curtains giving onto the entire Courthouse Square; that table was for Judge Mierck. A regular, Judge Mierck ate there four times a week. His belly told the tale, sagging down well beyond his waist; so did his skin, scored with broken veins as though all the burgundies he'd drunk were waiting in line to be flushed out. Mierck didn't like the prosecutor very much. The feeling was mutual. I might even be putting it too mildly. Yet we would see them greet each other solemnly, doffing their hats, like two men opposed in life's every matter who share its daily course all the same.

The oddest thing was that Destinat went so rarely to the Rébillon that his table remained unoccupied about three-quarters of the time. That caused Bourrache a fine loss of income, but he wouldn't have given that table to someone else for anything in the world, even on big fair days when all the farmers in the region, after a morning feeling the rumps of cows and drinking plum brandy by the litre, came to stuff themselves before going to ease themselves at Ma Nain's whorehouse. The table stayed unoccupied even as patrons were being turned away. Once Bourrache went so far as to eject a cattle trader who had dared to demand it. The man never came back.

'Better to have a king's table without the king than to seat somebody with manure all over his shoes!' That was Bourrache's explanation, one day when I was needling him.

2

The first Monday of December 1917 was freezing cold. The clatter of the ground under your heels could be felt reverberating up to your neck. The large blanket they'd thrown over the body was soaked in moments as the two coppers — Berfuche, a short guy with ears like a wild pig, hairs sticking out of them, and Grosspeil, an Alsatian whose family had emigrated forty years earlier — stood watching over it near the bank of the canal. A little further back stood young Bréchut. A boxy fellow with hair as stiff as broom straw, he was tugging at his waistcoat, not too sure what he ought to do: stay or leave. He was the one who'd spotted her in the water on his way to work at the port authority, where he kept the accounts. (He still does, only he's twenty years older now and every straw has fallen out of the broom.)

Lying on the ground, a ten-year-old's body seems even smaller, especially when it's saturated with winter water. Berfuche pulled back a corner of the blanket to confirm what he knew and puffed into his hands for warmth. Morning Glory's face appeared.

She looked like a fairy-tale princess with her eyelids blanched and lips turned blue, her hair entangled with the grass, withered brown by morning frosts. Her little hands had clutched at emptiness. It was so cold that day that all our moustaches whitened with hoarfrost as we huffed and stamped our feet like bulls getting ready to charge. In the sky some dim-witted geese were circling. They seemed to have lost their way. The sun huddled in his mantle of fog, which was fraying more and more. Even the cannon in the distance seemed to have frozen. You couldn't hear a thing.

'Maybe it's peace at last,' ventured Grosspeil.

'Peace, my arse!' his colleague snorted as he replaced the wet blanket over the little girl's body.

★ ★ ★

We were waiting for the gentlemen from V. Finally they arrived, accompanied by the mayor, who looked very much out of sorts, as you might too if you'd been jerked out of bed at the crack of dawn, especially in weather you wouldn't put a dog out in. There was Judge Mierck; his court clerk, whose name I never knew, though everyone called him

9

Crusty because of a nasty eczema that ate away at the left half of his face; three cocksure policemen; and a military officer. I don't know what he was doing there, but he didn't hang around for long; within moments he had keeled right over and we had to carry him to Jacques' Café. I figured the closest that slicker had ever come to a bayonet was in the armoury, and maybe not even then. You could tell from his flawlessly ironed uniform, tailored for a mannequin at Poiret's. He must have waged war beside a good cast-iron stove — sitting in a big velvet-upholstered armchair — and then in the evening telling young ladies in long gowns all about the action, under gilded mouldings and crystal chandeliers, among the bewigged musicians of a chamber orchestra, a glass of champagne in his hand.

Underneath his fancy Kronstadt hat and bon-vivant airs, Judge Mierck was a man of no feeling. All those wine sauces may have tinged his ears and nose, but they hadn't made him tender. He lifted the blanket himself and stared at Morning Glory for quite a while. The others were waiting for a word, a sigh: after all, he used to see her almost every day when he gorged himself at the Rébillon. He looked down at the little body as if it were a stone or a piece of driftwood that had been fished out, his eyes as icy as the water that flowed close by.

'It's Bourrache's youngest girl,' somebody murmured into his ear, in a tone that bespoke everything he wouldn't say. 'It's Bourrache's youngest girl,' somebody murmured into his ear, as though saying: *The poor little thing, she was just ten years old. You realise that only yesterday she was bringing you your bread and smoothing out your tablecloth.*

With a start, Judge Mierck rocked back on his heels towards the man who'd dared to address him. 'So what? I don't give a fuck. A corpse is a corpse!'

Before that moment we had all accepted Judge Mierck for what he was. He had his place and he held it, not liked much, but respected. On that first Monday of December, however, next to the drenched body of the little girl, his words, and even more how matter-of-factly he said them, almost cheerfully, with a gleam in his eyes at having a murder case at last, a real one, for it was murder, no doubt about it! — in this time of war, when all the killers had forsaken civil life so they could ply their aggression more violently in uniform — after that day, people in our region never thought of him without disgust.

'Well, well, well,' he said. As he surveyed

the scene he was humming, as if about to play skittles or go hunting. Then he realised he was hungry. It was just a whim, a caprice, but he *had* to have some eggs, boiled eggs — 'soft-boiled, not runny,' he specified — right away, there on the bank of the little canal, at ten degrees below zero, next to the body of Morning Glory. We were dumbfounded.

But it was an order, and one of the three policemen back from having dropped off the dandified officer jumped to and set off at the double to find the desired eggs 'More than eggs: little worlds, little worlds.' That's what Judge Mierck would say as he broke each shell with a tiny hammer of chased silver that he kept in his watch pocket for just this purpose, because the whim, which inevitably smeared his moustache with golden yolk, apparently came over him often.

As he waited for his eggs, he scrutinised the surroundings metre by metre, whistling to himself, his hands clasped behind his back, while the others kept trying to warm themselves. And he talked; he was not to be stopped from talking. In his mouth there was no more Morning Glory, though he too had called her that before; I had heard him myself. Now he said 'the victim', as though death — in addition to taking life — also took away the pretty names of flowers.

12

'Was it you who recovered the victim from the water?'

Young Bréchut dug into his waistcoat as though hoping to hide himself there. He nodded, causing the questioner to ask if the cat had got his tongue. Young Bréchut answered no, now shaking his head. This annoyed the judge, you could tell, and the good mood that the murder had furnished him began to dissolve, especially since it was taking a while for his eggs to arrive. Then young Bréchut offered some more details, and the judge listened, murmuring again from time to time, 'Well, well, well.'

The minutes passed. The cold lingered. The geese disappeared. The water continued flowing by. A corner of the blanket dipped into it; the current caught it and batted it back and forth like a hand keeping time. The judge didn't notice. He listened to Bréchut; in rapt attention, he'd forgotten the eggs.

The young man still had clear memories for now, but later he'd make a novel out of them, wending his way through every nearby café to tell the tale and be served drinks on the house. Towards midnight, dead drunk, he'd wind up bawling out the little girl's name, feverish tremolos, and pissing into his pants all the glasses of wine he'd downed along the way. By the very end of the evening,

13

he'd do no more than gesticulate before the roomful of regulars. Beautiful gestures, serious and dramatic, rendered even more eloquent by wine.

The fat buttocks of Judge Mierck melted down over his cane seat, a tripod in camel hide and ebony that had made a big impression on us the first few times he'd taken it out. 'Souvenir of the colonies': he'd spent three years chasing chicken thieves and grain poachers in Ethiopia or somewhere like that. He would fold and unfold it constantly at the scene of investigations, meditating on it like a painter before a model, brandishing it like a dandy, or slapping it against his side in the manner of a brigadier bracing himself for the charge.

The judge listened to Bréchut while eating his eggs, his 'little worlds', which had finally arrived, in a steaming white towel. The servile policeman who had fetched them stood to attention. When the shells had accumulated at the foot of his cane seat, the judge ground them with his heel while wiping his mouth with a big batiste handkerchief. You might have believed you were hearing the glass bones of some bird being broken. The crushed shells of the little worlds stuck to his boot like minuscule spurs, while nearby, only a few steps away, Morning Glory still lay

14

under the sodden wool.

Bréchut had ended his account. The judge consumed that too without difficulty. 'Well, well, well,' he said, getting up and straightening his shirtfront. He searched the landscape as though looking for his next thought. His hat had not budged.

The morning poured forth its light and its hours. All the men were set out like lead figures on a miniature stage. Berfuche's nose was red and his eyes weepy. Grosspeil took on the colour of the water. Crusty held his notebook, in which he'd already taken some notes, and sometimes as he scratched his sickly cheek the cold marbled it with white streaks. The egg bearer looked waxen. The mayor had left, very happy to return to the warmth of the town hall. He'd done his little duty; the rest didn't concern him.

The judge, no longer in a hurry, took a deep breath of the blue air, bouncing slightly with his hands behind his back. He was savouring the moment and the place as we waited for Victor Desharet, the doctor from V. He was trying to inscribe it in the deepest recesses of his memory, where there were already quite a few still lifes and murder landscapes. It was his personal museum; when he walked through it, I'm sure the thrills must have equalled those of the murderers. There's such a thin line between hunter and beast.

The doctor arrives: He and the judge make a fine pair. They've known each other since secondary school. They address each other as *tu*, but in their mouths the word is so curiously formed you might take it for the formal *vous*. They often have a meal together, at the Rébillon and other inns. It takes hours; they eat everything, but above all pork products and innards: head cheese, creamed tripe, breaded pig's feet, brains, fried kidneys. Having known each other for so long and wolfing down the same things, they've ended up looking rather alike: same complexion, same lavish folds under the neck, same belly, same eyes that seem to skim the world. They avoid seeing mud in the streets, just as they avoid seeing anything that in other men might provoke pity.

Desharet pronounces the corpse a textbook case. You can see he's worried about getting his gloves wet. And yet he too had known the little girl quite well. He touches the lips, raises the eyelids, exposes Morning Glory's neck, and there everyone catches a first sight of the purple blotches ringing it like a garland. 'Strangulation!' he declares.

The conclusion didn't require a university degree; all the same, on this frosty morning next to the small body, when the word was said we winced as if someone had slapped us.

'Well, well, well.' The judge seconds the observation, trying to contain his satisfaction at having his suspicion confirmed: a real case to sink his teeth into, a child murder to boot — a little girl, even. As he turns on his heel, his moustache fringed with yolk, he says with coquettish affectation, 'And this door, where does it lead?'

Everybody looks at it as though it has just appeared like a vision of the Virgin Mary: a little door ajar on the frozen trampled grass, an opening in a wide enclosure of high walls; behind these walls a park, a stately park with stately trees; and behind all these trees that interweave their naked branches, the outline of an imposing residence, a manor house, a great complex edifice.

It's Bréchut who answers, twisting his hands in the cold. 'It's the park of the château.'

'The château,' the judge repeats, in a mocking tone.

'Well, yes. Mr Prosecutor's château.'

'How about that? So that's the place . . . ' the judge said, more for himself than for us, who at that point meant as much to him as shrew-scat. He seemed rejuvenated to hear his rival invoked amid whiffs of a violent death — a powerful man like himself, whom he hated. Why, in fact, no one quite knew; but I was content to believe it simply the judge's nature.

He perked up, arranging his vast bulk on that exotic bum rest that he'd placed right across from the little door, at which he stared as if awaiting the start of a puppet show. He sat there a long time, while the rest of us tried to keep moving, stamping our feet and puffing into our gloves, until young Bréchut couldn't feel his nose and Crusty's cheek shaded over into greyish purple.

3

You have to admit that even for a château it's impressive. With its brick walls and slate roofs, it's the jewel of the ritzy part of town. Oh, yes, we do have one, as well as a hospital (that was always full in those years of worldwide slaughter); two schools, one for girls and one for boys; and the enormous factory, with its round stacks that pierce the sky, assailing it with plumes of smoke and clouds of soot, summer and winter, day and night. Since it was founded at the end of the 1880s, the factory has been the mainstay of the whole region. Few are the men who don't work there. Almost all of them have left their vineyards and fields for factory work. And ever since, brush and brambles have raced along the great hillsides, devouring the orchards, the vine stocks, and the furrows of good earth.

Our town isn't very big. It's not V, far from it. All the same, you could get lost here. By that I mean it contains enough shady nooks and belvederes that a soul can always find a place to nurse his melancholy moods. To the factory we owe the hospital, the schools, and the small library — which won't accept just any old book.

The factory owner doesn't have a name or a face; it's a group or, as the show-offs like to say, a consortium. Rows of houses have grown up in what was formerly a field of grain. Whole little streets of them, built one exactly like the next. Housing rented for a pretty penny or for nothing — in exchange for silence, obedience, public order — to workers who'd never hoped for so much and who found it pretty funny to be pissing in a toilet instead of through a black hole punched in a fir plank. The ancient farms, the few that still resist, clustered up against one another, tightly embracing the church as though by reflex — a hug of old walls and low windows — and exhaling from the cracked-open doors of their barns the sour smells of stables and curdled milk.

The owners even dug us two canals, one large and one small. The big one is for the barges that bring in coal and limestone and carry off the soda ash. The little one feeds the big one whenever it happens to need water. The construction went on for ten years or more. Gentlemen in ties went around everywhere, their pockets full of cash, and bought up land hand over fist. In those days you could avoid being sober for a month, they were buying so many rounds of drinks. Then one day you didn't see them anymore. They'd packed up and left. The town belonged to them. Everybody dried out. After that you had to work — for them.

Returning to the château, I'd honestly have to say it's the most imposing residence in town. Old Destinat — I mean the father — had built it just after the disaster of Sedan. And he hadn't cut corners. In our region, if you don't talk much, you may like to impress by other means. The prosecutor always lived there. He was born there, and there he would die.

The château is immense, beyond a human scale. Even more so since the family has never been a big one. Old Destinat, as soon as he had a son, halted production. His cup had overflowed — at least officially. The policy didn't prevent him from ballooning local bellies with some very handsome bastards, to whom he would give a gold coin and, on the day they reached twenty-one, a beautiful letter of reference — as well as a symbolic kick in the ass encouraging them to go far, far away and verify that the earth was truly round. Around here that's called generosity, but not everyone behaves that way.

The prosecutor was the last of the Destinats. There won't be any others. Not

21

that he wasn't married, but his wife died too soon, six months after their wedding, at which all the fame and fortune the region could muster had conspired to gather. The young lady was a de Vincey. Her ancestors had fought at Crécy. (Everybody else's too, no doubt, but in most cases nobody knows and nobody cares.)

I've seen a portrait of her, done just after her marriage, which hung in the entry hall of the château. The painter had come from Paris; he somehow captured her impending end in his depiction of her face. It was striking, the pallor of a woman soon to be dead, the resignation in her features. Her first name was Clélis, not common; it's very prettily engraved on the pink marble of her tomb.

An entire regiment could set up camp in the park of the château without feeling cramped. It's edged by water. At the far end there's a little communal path that serves as a shortcut between the town square and the port of embarkation; then comes the little canal of which I've spoken, over which the old man had a Japanese bridge built and daubed with paint. People call it the Blood Sausage, since it's the colour of cooked blood. On the far bank you can see the big windows of a high building, the factory lab, where the engineers figure out how to make more money for their bosses. A narrow and sinuous creek meanders along the eastern side of the park; it's called the Guerlante — 'Barely Slow' — a name that aptly expresses its lackadaisical flow, all whirlpools and water lilies. Here water permeates everything. The grounds of the château are like a huge soggy cloth; the grasses drip incessantly: it's a place to fall ill.

That's what happened to Clélis Destinat, and in just three weeks it was over, from the doctor's first visit to Ostrane's last shovelful of earth. He's the sexton and gravedigger, and he always pours that one out very slowly. 'Why that one and not the others?' I asked him one day. 'Because that one,' he said, looking at me with his eyes like dark wells, 'that one has to stick in people's memories.' Ostrane is a bit of a talker; he likes to say things for effect. He missed his calling. I could easily imagine him on the stage.

Old Destinat rose straight out of the dirt, but in fifty years he'd succeeded very well in cleaning himself off, thanks to many bank-notes and sacks of gold. He had come up in the world. He employed six hundred people, owned five tenant farms, eight hundred hectares of forest — all of it oak — pasturelands without end, ten residential buildings in

V, and a fine mattress of stocks — and no fly-by-nights, no Panama Canals! — on which ten men could have comfortably slept without elbowing one another.

He received and was received everywhere. Equally well at the bishop's and at the prefect's. He had become somebody.

I haven't spoken of Destinat's mother; she was something else again. She came from the best society — that of the land, but not from those who work it, rather those who have always owned it. As a dowry she had brought her enterprising husband more than half of what he would own and some good manners besides. Then she withdrew into books and needlework. She had the right to choose a first name for her son: it was Ange — Angel. The old man added Pierre; he found that Ange lacked gumption and manliness. After he was born, she didn't much see her son. From the English nannies of his early years to the Jesuit boarding school, time passed quicker than the bat of an eyelash. The mother had surrendered a whiner with pink skin and swollen eyes; one day she found before her a rather stiff young man, on whose chin three hairs grew between two pimples, and who like a true little gentleman — steeped in Latin, Greek, self-importance, and Casanova dreams — looked down his nose at her.

She died as she had lived, in the background. Few took note. The son was in Paris studying law. He came back for the burial even more of a young prig, now polished by the capital and its conversations, his walking stick of pale wood, his collar spotless and his lip surmounted by a thin moustache oiled à la Jaubert, the latest style! The old man ordered a gorgeous coffin from the cabinetmaker, who for the only time in his life got to work with rosewood and mahogany, before screwing on handles of real gold. A vault was built on which a bronze figure reaches towards the sky while another, kneeling, weeps in silence; it doesn't mean all that much, but it has quite a lovely effect.

After the period of mourning the old man hardly changed his habits, except for ordering from the tailor three suits made of black cloth, along with some crêpe armbands.

The day after the ceremony, the son returned to Paris. He would stay there for many years more.

Then one day he reappeared, now quite solemn, a prosecutor. He was no longer the young shit who'd thrown three roses on to his mother's coffin with a self-satisfied pout before immediately dashing off for fear of missing his train. It seemed that something had broken him from inside, bowed him down a bit. But we never knew what.

Later, being widowed broke him for good. It distanced him too: from the world, from us, no doubt from himself. I think he loved her, his young hothouse flower.

Old Destinat followed his wife after eight years, felled by a stroke on a footpath on his way to scold one of his tenant farmers, maybe even to throw him out. They found him with his mouth open and his nose smashed in the dense mud of early April. We owe this seasonal rite to the rains that lash the sky and mix the earth into a sticky paste. In the end he'd gone back to his origins; he'd come full circle. His money hadn't done that much for him. He'd died like a farmhand.

And now the son was truly alone. Alone in the great house.

Though he'd kept the habit of looking down his nose at the world, he made do with little. After his youth as a popinjay sporting fancy clothes and a foppish air, there was nothing left but an ageing man. His work consumed him entirely. In the father's time the château had employed six gardeners, a caretaker, a cook, three footmen, four chambermaids, and a chauffeur. This entire tribe, ruled with an iron rod, huddled in narrow common rooms and bedrooms under the eaves, where in winter the water froze in the jugs.

The prosecutor thanked one and all. He wasn't tight-fisted. He gave a handsome letter of recommendation and a tidy sum to each of them but kept only the cook, Barbe, who through force of circumstance became chambermaid as well, and her husband, who was known as Solemn because nobody had ever seen him smile — not even his wife, who for her part always wore a joyous puckered face. Solemn busied himself as best he could with the upkeep of the estate, in addition to all manner of minor tasks. The couple went out rarely. You could hardly hear them — or, in fact, the prosecutor. The house seemed to be asleep. The roof of a turret leaked. A big wisteria, allowed to spread, smothered several shutters with its branches. Some quoins cracked under the frost. The château aged just as human beings do.

Destinat never received anyone at home. He had turned his back on everything. Every Sunday he went to mass. He had his pew, with the initials of the family carved into the oaken plank. He never missed a service. The priest gazed at him fondly during sermons as though he were a cardinal or other manner of accomplice. And then at the end of mass, once the flock with their caps and embroidered shawls had left his lair, the priest escorted him outside to the square. Below the pealing bells, as Destinat pulled on his kid gloves — his hands were delicate like a lady's, with fingers as slender as cigarette holders — they spoke of trivial things, but in the tones of those who know, one owing to the service of souls, the other to sizing them up. The ballet was performed. Then Destinat and the priest parted, and it was up to each man to comprehend his solitude and furnish it a gloss.

★   ★   ★

One day, one of the factory directors came to request the honour of being received at the château: protocol, exchange of cards, bowing and scraping, hat doffed, and, at last, admission. This director was a fat jolly Belgian, with curly red sideburns and stubby legs; he was dressed like a gentleman from a novel, in a short jacket and checked trousers, with braid trim and polished jodhpur boots. In brief: Barbe arrives with a large tray and all the paraphernalia for tea. She serves them. She disappears. The director chatters on. Destinat hardly speaks, scarcely drinks, doesn't smoke, doesn't laugh, listens politely. The other one beats around the bush, talks about billiards for ten long minutes, then partridge-shooting, bridge, Havana cigars, and finally French gastronomy. This makes three-quarters of an hour already that he's been there. He's getting ready to broach the weather, but Destinat suddenly glances at his watch, sidelong yet lingering, to grant his guest the leisure of observing him.

The director understands, coughs, sets his cup down, coughs again, picks it up, and finally tests the water: He has a favour to ask but is not sure if he should dare; he hesitates; in fact, he fears being troublesome, even rude. All the same he ends up taking the plunge: The château is big, very big, and there are the outbuildings, particularly that little house in the park, uninhabited but charming, off on its own. The director's problem is that the factory is doing well — too well — and consequently needs more and more personnel: above all, engineers, managers. But there's nowhere to accommodate these managers, because, you understand, we can't put them in the settlements, in the workers' houses; no, can't make them rub elbows with people who sometimes sleep four to a bed, who drink plonk, who swear every tenth word, who breed like animals, never! And so an idea has occurred to the director, just an idea. If the prosecutor would agree — but nothing obliges him to, of course; everyone is master of his own home — but after all, if he would agree to rent the little house in the park, the factory and the director would be so grateful to him, they would obviously pay a premium, and they wouldn't place just anyone there, only top-notch people, polite, discreet, quiet, assistant managers if not managers, and without children — he the director gives his word — as he sweats profusely in his false collar and jodhpur boots. He stops talking and waits; he doesn't even dare to go on looking at Destinat, who has risen to contemplate the park and the fog that wraps around itself.

There's a silence that won't break. The director is already regretting his initiative when, abruptly, Destinat turns around and tells him all right. Just like that. With a blank voice. The other man can't get over it. He bows, stammers, mumbles, thanks him with polite flourishes, retreats walking backwards, then leaves before his host changes his mind.

Why did the prosecutor agree? Perhaps simply so the director would be on his way that day, leaving Destinat to his silence once again. Or perhaps he'd taken pleasure in the fact that, for once in his life, someone had asked him for something — something other than a sentence of death or mercy.

4

This was in 1897 or 1898 — thereabouts. A long time ago. The factory paid for the renovation of the little house in the park, gnawed at by humidity like the hold of an old ship. Up till now whatever was unneeded had been stored there, a hotchpotch of this and that: dislodged armoires and rat traps, rusty scythes thin as crescent moons, stones, slates, a tilbury carriage, broken toys, skeins of twine, garden tools, tattered clothes. Also a bunch of stags' antlers and wild boars' heads, all quite dead and stuffed. The old man had been a fanatical hunter; the son, who also made heads roll, detested seeing them and so had had these trophies tossed there in a heap. Spiders had woven many a web over them, giving the whole collection an antique patina, redolent of sarcophagi and Egyptian mysteries. To spruce the place up after the main work was completed, a decorator came specially from Brussels.

The first tenant arrived as soon as the renovation was complete. The second replaced him six months later, and then that one left in turn, whereupon a third showed up, and then a fourth, and so on. Everyone lost track. Many would pass through; none would stay more than a year, and each resembled the last. People stopped trying to distinguish them. They would say, 'Look, there's the tenant going by!' They were overgrown boys, still fairly young, who made no noise, never went out, never brought a woman back, and always stuck to business. They'd head for the factory at seven, return at eight after a supper eaten in the big building known to us as the Casino — I wonder why, since no one has ever played any sort of game there! — which served as a canteen for all the engineers. Sometimes a few of them dared to go for a brief stroll, of a Sunday, in the park. Destinat said nothing. He would watch them from behind his curtains and wait for them to go away before taking a walk himself and settling down on a bench.

The years passed. Destinat's life seemed an unchanging ritual played out between the courthouse of V, the cemetery where each week he visited his wife's grave, and the château in which he resided: shut in as though invisible, withdrawn from the world, which wove around him, bit by bit, a cloak of forbidding legend.

He advanced in years, but he remained the same — in appearance, at any rate. Always this severity, which inspired chills, and this silence, which seemed as long and complicated as a century. If you wanted to hear his voice — which by the way was very soft — all you had to do was attend a trial. They took place often. Murder is more common around here than elsewhere. Maybe that's because the winters are long and people get bored, and the summers are so hot they make the blood boil in your veins.

The jurors didn't always understand what the prosecutor meant: he'd read too much, and they hadn't read enough. Among them you saw all kinds, though seldom bigwigs; mostly they were nobodies: rancid craftsmen cheek by jowl with ruddy-faced farmers, civil servants, priests in worn cassocks who'd come from their country parish having risen before the sun, hauliers, exhausted workmen. All sat on the same bench, the good one. Many could just as well have found themselves on the opposite bench, between the two moustachioed bailiffs, stiff as pokers. And I'm sure each vaguely sensed this in his heart of hearts, realised it without wanting to admit it to himself, and that's what often made them so full of peremptory hate towards the man they had to judge: their brother in bad luck or in fortitude.

When Destinat's voice could be heard in the courtroom, all murmurs ceased. The whole room seemed to check itself, as when you stop before a mirror and pull on your shirt tail to make the collar stand straight; the room was looking at itself and holding its breath. Into this silence, the prosecutor would fling his opening remarks. They tore into the silence, Never more than five little sheets, whatever the case, whoever the accused. The prosecutor's trick was simplicity itself. No swagger. A cold and meticulous depiction of the murder and the victim, that's all. But that in itself is a lot, especially when you don't omit a single detail. Most often, the medical examiner's report was his gospel. He insisted on it. It was enough for him to read it out, his voice dwelling on the most trenchant particulars. He wouldn't gloss over a single wound, not a gash, not the least laceration, much less a sliced throat or gaping belly. All of a sudden the public and the jurors would see before them images from far away, from the darkest underside, the emerging face of evil and its metamorphoses.

It's often said that we fear what we don't know. But I say fear is born when one day we learn what we were unaware of only the night before. That was Destinat's secret: offhandedly, he would slip thoughts of things they didn't want to live with under the noses of those complacent louts. The rest was child's play. He could ask for the head, and the jury would serve it to him on a silver platter.

After that, he would go and have lunch at the Rébillon. 'Another one cut down to size, Mr Prosecutor!' Bourrache would show him to his table and pull out his chair for him with flourishes fit for a lord. Destinat would lay out the silverware, clink the knife handle against his glass. Judge Mierck would greet him mutely, and Destinat would return his greeting in kind. The two of them sat less than ten metres apart, each at his own table. Yet they never exchanged a word. Mierck ate messily, like a pig, his napkin tied around his neck like a stable groom, his fingers greasy with sauce, and his eyes already clouded by wine-vapour nymphs. As for the prosecutor, he was, as I say, well-bred. He cut his fish as though caressing it. The rain was still falling. Judge Mierck would gobble down his desserts. Morning Glory would be dozing near the great hearth, lulled by fatigue and the dancing of the flames. The prosecutor would linger in the folds of his own vapid dream.

Already, somewhere, a blade was being sharpened, a scaffold being raised.

★   ★   ★

35

I've been told that Destinat's talents and fortune could have taken him far. Instead, he planted himself for all his days in our town — in other words, nowhere — in a region where for years life reached us only as the murmur of a distant music, until one fine day it all crashed down on our heads and battered us horribly for a span of four years.

The portrait of Clélis still adorned the entry hall of the château. Her smile watched the world change and sink into the abyss. She wore the garments of a light-hearted time that was no more. Over the years her pallor had disappeared, and the discoloured varnishes shaded her cheeks a lukewarm pink. Each day Destinat passed by beneath her, a little more worn, himself only more faded, his gestures slowed and his gait more deliberate. The two of them moved even further away from each other. Brutally, death spirits beautiful things away and yet keeps them intact. That is its true grandeur. We can't fight it.

Destinat so loved time that he could relish simply watching it go by, sometimes doing no more than sitting behind a window, on a rattan chaise longue, or else on the bench on top of a low manmade mound, covered with anemones and periwinkles, overlooking the lazy waters of the Guerlante and the more

36

hurried stream of the small canal. At such times you might have taken him for a statue.

For many years I've tried to understand, though I don't think of myself as any smarter than the next guy. I grope along, I get lost, I go round in circles. At the beginning, before the Case, Destinat was a name to me, an official position, a house, a fortune, a figure I came across at least two or three times a week and to whom I tipped my hat. But what lay behind all that I had no way of knowing. Since then, by living with his ghost, it's a little as if he were an old acquaintance, a relative in misfortune, a part of myself, so to speak, and I do my best to make him talk and come alive again, so I might ask him a question. Only one. Now and then I tell myself that I'm wasting my time: the man is as impenetrable as morning fog, and a thousand evenings wouldn't be time enough for me to see my way through. But now I have time to spare. It's as if I'm outside the world. All the hurly-burly seems so far off. I live in the movements of a history no longer mine. Little by little, I steal away.

5

1914. There was, in our town, on the eve of the great slaughter, a sudden scarcity of engineers. The factory kept running as ever, but something compelled the Belgians to stay home in their little kingdom, under the spindly shadow of their operetta monarch. The prosecutor was informed, with many bows and courteous words that there would be no more tenants.

The summer had announced itself as a hot one, under the arbours and inside the skulls of the many patriots who in their fervour had been wound up tight as fine clockwork. Everywhere they raised their fists and bared their painful memories. Around here, as all over, wounds have a hard time closing, especially when they never dry and are left to fester in evenings of brooding and rancour. Out of pride and stupidity, a whole country was ready to fight it out with another country. The fathers drove their sons. The sons drove their fathers. Hardly anyone other than the women — mothers, wives, sisters — could see all this with even an inkling of coming misery, a foresight that projected them well beyond those afternoons of joyous shouts, of glasses tossed back, of rounds of songs that pounded against the canopy of the chestnut trees until your ears rang.

Actually, our little town could hear the war but didn't wage it. You could even say without giving offence that we lived off it: our men kept the factory going. It was needed. An order was handed down from on high — a good one for once. By dispensation of I forget which far-off government bureaucrat, all workers were reserved for essential civilian service. And so at least eight hundred strapping local lads would escape the raging guns and the perils of the front line. Eight hundred men, who in the eyes of some were never men at all, who rose each morning from a warm bed and a drowsy embrace rather than from a muddy trench, to go haul useful things rather than cadavers. The incessant blast of shells; the dread of meeting the fate of so many others; of having buddies caught in barbed wire just twenty metres away, left to groan until they died, when the rats would set upon their remains — all that stayed far away. Instead, there was life pure and simple: real life. It unfolded each morning, not as a dream somewhere beyond the fumes but as a warm certainty that smells of sleep and women.

Lucky bastards! Deadbeats! That's what all the convalescent soldiers thought — one-eyed, legless, amputated, crushed, gassed, mangled, faces smashed — as they passed the workers on our streets, in the pink of health, about to open their lunch boxes. Some, with an arm in a sling or dragging a wooden leg, would turn around and spit on the ground when those men went by. You could understand it. A person can hate you for less than that.

Not everybody was a civilian worker. The few farmers who were not too young or too old traded their pitchforks for rifles. Leaving as proud conscripts, they couldn't have known that soon enough they would have their names engraved on a monument still to be built.

And then there was a departure notable for its ceremony: that of the schoolteacher, whose name was Fracasse — 'Crash' — a name you could hardly believe. He wasn't from around here. A proper farewell was organised. The children had composed a little song, very moving and innocent, which brought tears to his eyes. The city council presented him with a tobacco pouch and a fancy pair of gloves. I really wonder what he could have done with those gloves of exquisite salmon-coloured silk; when he removed them from their sharkskin box and tissue paper, he looked at them incredulously. I don't know what became of Fracasse: dead, wounded, or else safe and sound after the four years. In any case, he never came back, which I can understand. The war not only turned out dead men by the ton, it also cut the world and all our memories in two, as though everything that had taken place before was crammed into a paradise at the bottom of some old pocket you'd never dare reach into again.

They sent a substitute teacher, too old to be mobilised. I remember his madman's eyes above all, two steel balls in oyster white. 'I'm opposed!' he said from the first, when the mayor came to show him his classroom. We called him Opposed. It's all well and good to be opposed, but opposed to what? We never found out. In any case, three months and it all came to a head, though the guy had undoubtedly started losing his grip a long time before that. Sometimes he would break off the lesson, stare at the children, and go *rat-a-tat-tat* like a tommy gun, or else he would ape a falling shell by dropping to the floor and remaining motionless for minutes on end. He was alone in this plight. Madness is a land that's not open to day-trippers; it has to be booked in advance. As for him, he arrived there in style, having lifted anchor, cast off, and sunk with all the panache of a captain who goes down with his ship, upright at the prow.

Each evening he would go bobbing and skipping along the canal. He talked to himself, usually words that nobody understood, stopping now and then to battle an invisible adversary with a hazel-wood stick. Then he would set off bobbing again, murmuring, 'Tagada Tagada T'soin T'soin!'

He crossed the line on a day of huge bombardments. The windowpanes were trembling every five seconds, like the surface of water under a strong north wind. The stench reached even into our homes. We stuffed the cracks in the windows with damp rags. The children would later recount that Opposed — after almost an hour of sitting with his head between his hands, pressing so hard it nearly burst — had stood up on his desk and methodically removed his clothes while singing the Marseillaise at the top of his lungs. And then, naked as Adam, he ran over to the flag and threw it on the floor. After pissing on it, he tried to set it on fire. At that point young Jeanmaire, the biggest boy in class — he was going on fifteen — calmly got up and subdued him with a cast-iron poker to the forehead.

'The flag, it's sacred!' the kid said later,

very proudly, when everyone crowded around to hear him explain his feat. He had that streak in him already. He would die three years later at Chemin des Dames. Also on account of the flag.

When the mayor arrived the teacher was stretched out, still completely naked, on the sodden, slightly burnt tricolour, his hair a bit singed from the fire that hadn't really caught. Two orderlies took him in a straitjacket that made him look like a fencer, the purple lump on his brow like some bizarre emblem of office. He didn't speak, quiet as a scolded child. I think by then he was completely unhinged.

The fact remained that the school was now without a teacher, and though the kids were pleased, this didn't sit well with the local authorities, who couldn't afford to fall behind in brain-washing the young and miss turning out their quota of recruits. After all, once the first illusions had passed — 'Those Krauts, in two weeks we'll make them eat Berlin!' — nobody knew how long the war would last, and a reserve force seemed only sensible.

The mayor was on the verge of tearing his hair out; he went on a crusade, but none of that changed a thing: He could find no solution, any more than he could find a replacement for Fracasse.

And then the solution appeared just like that — on 13 December, 1914, to be exact — in the mail-coach that came from V. It stopped as usual across from the Quentin-Thierry hardware store, where the window always displayed the same boxes of rivets in every size, alongside mole traps. We saw four livestock traders elbowing one another as they got out, red as cardinals from having drunk too much in toasting their latest transaction. Then two women, widows who made the trip to town to sell their cross-stitch needlework; and old man Berthiet, a lawyer, retired from his paperwork, who repaired once a week to a back room of the Excelsior Grand Café for a game of bridge, with some other leftovers of his ilk. There were also three girls returned from having made the wedding purchases for the one among them who was a bride-to-be. And then finally, at the very last, when it seemed there was nobody left, we saw a young lady get off. At that moment the sound of gunfire and shell bursts seemed to cease. Wafting on the air was something of the warmth of autumn and the sap of ferns.

She looked deliberately to the right and then to the left, as if to see what sort of place she was stepping into. Her two small, brown leather bags with copper clasps had preceded her. Her clothing was simple, without frill or ornament. She bent over slightly, grasped the two little bags, and, striking a slender outline that the evening swathed in a gauzy mist of blue and pink, disappeared from view.

In her name, which we would later learn, that of a flower seemed to drowse: Lysia. It suited her well, as a long gown might have done. She had not yet turned twenty-two; she came from the north, just passing through; her family name was Verhareine.

Her little circuit out of our view led her to Augustine Marchoprat's haberdashery. She asked for directions to the town hall and the mayor's house; yes, that's what the young lady had requested 'with a voice sweet as honey', the dried-up prunes would later recall. And old Mrs Marchoprat, that gossip, immediately closed her door, pulled the iron grating down, and ran to report to her dear friend Mélanie Bonnipeau, a pious bonneted biddy who spent most of her time scanning the street from her low window, among green plants that uncoiled their aqueous curls against the windowpanes, her fat neutered cat with the head of a solemn monk settled on her lap. The two old ladies set about spinning their themes, unfurling plots borrowed from the penny novels they often devoured on winter evenings, rehashing all the episodes till they were even more asinine and preposterous. Louisette, the mayor's

45

maid, a girl as simple as a goose, passed by half an hour later.

'So who is she?' old mother Marchoprat asks her.

'Who is who?'

'The girl with the two bags!'

'A girl from the north.'

'From the north? What north?' the shopkeeper continues.

'I don't know, from the north. There's only one.'

'And what does she want?'

'She wants the job.'

'What job?'

'Fracasse's job.'

'She's a schoolteacher?'

'That's what she says.'

'And the mayor, what did he say?'

'Oh, he was all smiles.'

'I'm not surprised.'

'He told her, 'You've saved me!''

''You've saved me'?'

'Yes just like I said.'

'There's another one with ideas in his head.'

'What ideas?'

'My dear girl, ideas in his trousers, if you prefer. You know your master, he's a man!'

'But what kind of ideas are inside trousers — '

'My God, she's a fool! And your bastard, how did you acquire him, from a puff of air?'

Clever enough to take offence at least, Louisette turned her back on them and left. The two old ladies were pleased. They had fodder for the evening: the north, men and their vices, and the young girl, too beautiful, altogether too beautiful, to be a teacher — beautiful enough to have no profession at all.

By the following day we knew everything, or almost.

Lysia Verhareine had been put up in the largest room of the only hotel in town, at the expense of the mayor's office. And the mayor, dressed like a young bridegroom, had come in the morning to pick her up to introduce her all around and escort her to the school. You should have seen him, waltzing around till he almost split the seams of his Sunday-best jasper-black trousers, the pirouettes of his hundred kilos graceful as a circus elephant on its hind legs. Beside him the young lady was gazing all the while far beyond the landscape, even while she shook our hands one by one with a gentle squeeze from her slender fingers, as though she sought to wing her way into the distance, to lose herself there.

She entered the school and surveyed the

47

empty classroom as if it were a battlefield. The place stank of country children. A few ashes from the burned flag still remained on the floor. Several overturned chairs gave the place an air of high jinks just ended. Observing the scene from outside with a nose pressed to the windowpanes, one could make out the first lines of a poem written on the blackboard:

No doubt their naked hearts have felt
The biting cold, and halfway death
Under the open stars . . .

The words stopped abruptly. The handwriting, which must have belonged to Opposed, was still there to remind us of his mad eyes and gymnastics, though by now he must have been lying on a flea-infested mattress who knows where, or shivering under a regimen of cold showers and mauve electric shocks.

The mayor had made some remarks after opening the door and pointing out the flag; then he stuck his sausage fingers into the pockets of his silk waistcoat and preened in silence, casting a dour glance our way from time to time — which meant, no doubt, Well, what are you doing there, you people? Why don't you get the hell out of here and make yourselves useful? But none of us left. We were drinking in the scene like a glass of rare wine.

The young woman took tiny steps about the room, to the right, to the left, and up to the desks, where notebooks and pens still lay neatly in place. She leaned over one desk and read the page of writing; we saw her smile. At the same time, we saw her golden hair, cascading on her neck like sea-foam, between the collar of her blouse and her bare skin. Next she stopped before the ashes of the flag, righted two fallen chairs, matter-of-factly arranged some dry flowers in a vase, and without remorse erased the unfinished verses from the blackboard. She smiled at the mayor, who was nailed to the ground where he stood, stunned by this twenty-one-year-old's smile, while less than fifteen leagues away they were slicing one another's throats with naked blades, scared shitless, falling by the thousands each day, far from any feminine smile, on ravaged earth where even the idea of woman had become a chimera, a drunkard's dream, an insult altogether too beautiful.

The mayor patted his belly to give himself an air of distinction. Lysia Verhareine walked out of her classroom, her steps worthy of a dance.

6

The teacher had always been lodged above
the school: three tidy rooms facing due south,
overlooking the hillside and its mantle of
grapevines and mirabelle orchards. Fracasse
had made a pretty place of it, a nook redolent
of bees-wax, bound books, meditation and
bachelorhood. I had seen it on occasion, one
or two evenings when we had chatted about
this and that, each of us a little reserved. No
one had gone there since Opposed had
succeeded him — and not even subsequently,
after the orderlies had taken the madman
away.

The mayor had the key in the lock, but he
had a hard time pushing the door open. He
was a bit nonplussed at the resistance of the
swollen timbers; and by the time he got in, his
fine tour-guide smile had vanished: or so I
suppose. I'm reconstituting the story, filling
in the gaps. But I don't think I'm inventing
much, since we all remarked the anguish
beaded on his forehead in fat drops of sweat
and surprise, his choked redness when he
came back outside a few minutes later to get
some air in deep desperate gulps, as he

collapsed against the wall. From his pocket he drew a big checked handkerchief — not very clean — and mopped himself with it, like the peasant he'd never ceased to be.

A good while later, Lysia Verhareine also came out again into the daylight; it made her squint, an agreeable effect, as she smiled in our direction. She moved a few steps away from us and knelt down to pick up two late chestnuts that had just hit the ground, bursting from their burrs wonderfully fresh, all shiny and brown. She rolled them in her hands and sniffed them with her eyes closed, and after that she gently departed. We rushed up the stairs to see, elbowing one another all the way; it was an apocalypse.

Nothing remained of the small apartment's former charm, absolutely nothing. Opposed had methodically devastated the place, the meticulousness of destruction carried to the extreme of cutting each book in the library into one-centimetre squares — Lepelut, a pencil pusher who was a stickler for precision, measured them before our eyes — and whittling the furniture with a penknife, piece by piece, until he had reduced it all to huge blond hills of wood shavings. Remains of meals in scattered mounds had attracted insects of every kind. On the floor, dirty linens mimicked fleshless bodies, broken and recumbent. And on the walls, on all the walls, in finely shaped letters, the verses of the Marseillaise were inscribed, their bellicose harangues unfurling across the wallpaper with its pattern of daisies and hollyhocks. The madman had written and rewritten those verses, demented litanies that gave us all the impression of being shut up between the pages of an atrocious book. And he'd traced each letter with his fingertips, fingertips dipped in his own filth, which he'd apparently shat in every corner of the rooms every day he'd spent with us — after his exercise perhaps, or amid the unnerving boom of the guns alongside the unbearable song of the birds and the obscene perfume of the honeysuckle, lilacs, and roses, under the blue of the sky, stirred by the sweet wind.

Opposed had ended up going to war after all — after his own fashion, at least. With strokes of razor, knife, and excrement, he had drawn up his private battlefield, his trench, his hell. And he too had wailed in agony before it swallowed him up.

It's true that the place reeked to high heaven; but the mayor was a total cream puff too, without heart, without guts, less than a man. The young teacher on the other hand was a real lady: she had left the apartment without shuddering, without passing judgement. She had looked up at the sky and its transit of fumes and bulbous clouds; she'd taken a few steps, picked up two chestnuts, and caressed them as though they were the madman's feverish temples, as though they were his wan forehead, ashen with all the deaths, with all the tortures accumulated during our long humanity, with all our putrid wounds open for centuries and next to which the smell of shit is nothing — no, nothing but the faint, sour and sickly hint of a body still living, *living*, which shouldn't in any way revolt us, shame us, much less destroy us.

The fact remained, however, that she couldn't occupy the apartment. The mayor was soon three sheets to the wind, having knocked back his sixth absinthe in a single gulp, without waiting for the sugar to dissolve, as he had done with the five before; he was recovering, I suppose, from his close encounter with the blackness that lurks in us all. The unexpected rendezvous had led him straight to the Thérieux Café (the nearest one), towards which the rest of us eventually ambled, still shaking our heads thinking about the lunatic's calligraphy, his universe of confetti and stains. Before long, we too were in our cups (though more out of boredom than terror) and shrugging our shoulders, as through the narrow window we watched the east darkening to inky blackness.

And then, amid all his snoozing and snoring, swilling and swaggering, the mayor's chair finally collapses under him, taking the table with it. A good laugh all around, and a round of drinks too. Words flow again. We're talking and talking when one of us, I don't remember who, brings up the subject of Destinat. And another — again the exact one escapes me — proposes matter-of-factly, 'That's where they should put the little teacher, over at the prosecutor's house in the park — where the tenant was.'

Everybody found this a fine idea, not least the mayor, who allowed that the thought had already crossed his mind. A wave of rib-poking and knowing glances rippled through the rest of us. It was late. The church bell clanged twelve strokes against the night. The wind blew a shutter back. Outside, the rain tussled with the ground like a big river.

7

By the next day, the mayor had moderated his grandeur. Humbled in dress as well as demeanour, he was back in his accustomed thick corduroys, wool jacket, otter-skin cap, and hobnailed boots. The finery and self-assurance of the bridegroom had been consigned to oblivion. His playacting, the preening of the coxcomb, was of no use now: Lysia Verhareine had discerned his soul. Besides, calling on the prosecutor in evening dress was bound to rub him the wrong way from the outset. No one likes a suppliant with airs, and Destinat would have regarded the mayor as you might regard a monkey wearing a man's clothes.

The little teacher kept her faraway smile. Her dress was never more formal than it had been on the first day, but it assumed the forest shades of autumn, trimmed with a Bruges lace that lent her garb a religious gravity. As the mayor led the way, floundering in the muddy streets, she placed her tiny feet on the water-furrowed earth, avoiding every puddle and rivulet as if she were playing at tracking a gentle animal in the sodden ground. Beneath her smooth, young-girl's features, you could still make out the mischievous child she must have been not long ago, leaving off hopscotch to slip into gardens and pick bunches of cherries and redcurrants.

She waited before the steps leading up to the château as the mayor went in alone to present his request to Destinat. The prosecutor received him in the entrance hall, the two standing all the while under the ten-metre-high ceiling, in the chill of the black-and-white marble tiles on the floor that described a game begun at the dawn of time, in which ordinary men are pawns, in which the rich, the powerful, and the warlike make their moves while from afar, always failing, the servants and starvelings watch.

The mayor played the only card he could: directness. With his eyes lowered to the tiles and Destinat's spats (cut from first-class calfskin), he declared himself without mincing his words. He hid nothing: the shitty Marseillaise, the cataclysmic mess, and the idea that had occurred to everyone — first of all to him — of accommodating the girl in the house in the park. Then he fell silent and waited, groggy as an animal that has run smack into a fence or a big oak trunk.

The prosecutor didn't reply. He gazed

56

through the cathedral glass of the great door at the light as it came and went, in all tranquillity; then he made the mayor understand that he wished to see the young woman, and the door was opened to Lysia Verhareine.

I could embroider: that's not hard, of course. But what would be the point? The truth is so much stronger when you look it in the face. Lysia entered and held out her hand to Destinat; it was so slender he didn't see it at first, busy as he was in examining the young woman's shoes — slight summer pumps in black leather and crêpe, both daubed with mud at the heel and the toe. He would have noticed even had this mud, more grey than brown, not left its smudges on the floor, lightening the black squares and darkening the white.

The prosecutor was known for keeping his shoes as shiny as the helmet of a Republican guard, no matter what the weather. A metre of snow might fall, it could rain cats and dogs, the street could disappear under the mud, but that man would keep his feet shod in immaculate leather. I had seen him brushing them off one day, in the hallway of the courthouse, when he believed that no one was observing him — while a little further on, behind walnut panelling darkened by the years, twelve jurors were considering the weight of a man's head. That day there was a hint of disdain mixed with horror in his gestures, and a lot became clear to me. Destinat detested stains, even the most earthly and natural. A shudder habitually seized him when he surveyed the splattered clodhoppers of the prisoners who ganged together on the courtroom benches, or of the men and women he passed in the street. The state of your shoes revealed whether you were worthy to be looked in the eyes or not. And everything depended on a perfect polish, on whether he beheld a gleam like a bald pate after a summer of bright sun or, instead, a crust of dried earth, the dust of the roads, the mottling where a burst of rain had left its mark on the hard sunken leather.

But there, in front of the tiny shoes spattered with mud that had altered the marble chessboard of the universe, something was different: it was as though the forward march of the world had ground to a halt, the mechanism jammed.

Finally, Destinat took the small proffered hand into his own and held it a long time. A very long time.

'An eternity,' the mayor told us later. 'And a long one at that!' he added. Then he continued, 'The prosecutor wouldn't let go of that hand. He kept holding it in his, and his eyes — you should have seen them — were no longer his. Even his lips: they were moving, or trembling a bit, but nothing came out. He stared at the girl as if he'd never seen a woman, not one like that, anyway. As for me, I could not have felt more superfluous, with those two lost in each other's eyes — because the girl for her part didn't blink, she didn't bow her head; there was not the least shyness or embarrassment, just her pretty smile, which she shot at him with no let-up. Really, the dumb fuck in the story is me, looking for some way to justify my presence; that's when I took refuge in the big portrait of his wife, in those folds of her dress that fall all the way to her feet. What else could I do? Finally, it was the girl who withdrew her hand — but not her gaze — and the prosecutor looked at his palm, as though he'd touched the Holy Rood. After a silence, he glanced at me and said yes — that's all, a simple yes. Beyond that, I don't know.'

He did know very well, no doubt, but it no longer mattered. He and Lysia Verhareine left the château. Destinat remained, standing a long while in the place where he'd received them. And then at last he went back up to his apartments with a heavy step; I have that from Solemn, who'd never seen him so stooped before, so sluggish and dazed. When the old servant asked if everything was all right, Destinat didn't even answer. Perhaps he returned to the entrance hall that very evening, with no light but the penumbra of the phosphorescent blue streetlights, to convince himself of what he had seen, to look for the delicate traces of mud on the black-and-white tile, which Barbe had dutifully wiped away, and then to search the eyes of his wife: she was smiling too, but a smile from former days that nothing could light up now, and which seemed as far from him as anything could be.

★ ★ ★

It was then that strange days began.

The war was still going on, perhaps more evident than ever; the roads became furrows of some endless anthill, a shade of grizzled beards. The guns now boomed incessantly, day and night, and the noise marked out our existences like a macabre clock, sweeping up the shattered bodies and lost lives with its vast hand. The worst part is that we ended up almost not hearing it any longer. Every day we would see men walking by, young men, always in the same direction, still believing they could cheat death. They smiled, not knowing what they didn't yet know. In their eyes was the light of their former life. Only the sky could remain pure and gay, indifferent to the rot and evil being spread across the earth, under its dome of stars.

And so the young teacher settled into the small house in the park of the château. It suited her better than anyone else. She made it into a frame for her own image, where the breeze would enter without being invited and caress the pale blue curtains and the bouquets of wildflowers arranged on the windowsill. She spent long hours smiling — at what, no one knew — beside her window or on the bench in the park, with a little notebook of red morocco in her hands; her eyes seemed to meet the horizon, always going beyond it towards a point scarcely visible, or perhaps visible to the heart rather than the eyes.

It didn't take us long to adopt her. Our town isn't the most welcoming to strangers, maybe even less to ones of the female sex. But she managed to win everyone over with little things, and even those who might have been her rivals — I mean the young ladies prospecting for a husband — were soon greeting her with a slight nod, which she returned with the light-hearted vivacity that enlivened everything she did.

The pupils were open-mouthed at seeing

her, which surprise she mocked gently without malice. Never had school been so fully or joyously attended. Fathers had a hard time keeping their sons at home; they balked at the slightest chores, and each day away from their desks seemed like a long boring Sunday.

Every morning Martial Maire, a simpleton who'd lost half his head under an ox's hoof, placed a bouquet before her classroom door. When there weren't any flowers for him to pick, he'd leave a handful of scented herbs releasing the minty odour of wild thyme, the sugary scent of lucerne. Sometimes, when he could find neither grasses nor flowers, he might leave three pebbles he'd carefully washed in the big village spring in rue Pachamort, wiping them dry on his ragged woollen jersey. Always he would hurry away before she discovered his offering. Some girls would have laughed at such a loon; they would have swept away the pebbles and the grasses. But Lysia picked them up carefully, as her charges lined up before her, motionless, gazing at her rosy cheeks, her hair of blonde verging on amber. She held the offering of the day like a baby chick, and as soon as she had entered the classroom, she'd put it with all ceremony in its special place: if flowers or herbs, in a small blue ceramic vase shaped like a cygnet; if pebbles, along the edge of her desk. Martial Maire would be watching from outside. She'd give him a smile — and off he'd run. At times, when she came across him on the street, she would stroke his forehead as you might to detect a fever, and he would swoon at the warmth of her touch.

More than one might have loved to take that simpleton's place. In some sense, Maire was their stake in a common dream. The young woman soothed him like a child, and he awaited her as would a young fiancé. No one ever thought of making fun of them.

8

And Destinat? That's another question; there things turn murky again. Perhaps Barbe was better informed than any of us. Years later, long after the Case, long after the war, she would come talk to me about him. Everybody was dead, Destinat in 1921, the others too, and there was little point in sifting the ashes any more. But she told me, all the same: at the end of an afternoon, in front of the small house to which she'd retired, with other widows like herself. Solemn had been run over in 1923 by a cart he hadn't heard coming. Barbe found her consolation in chatter and brandied cherries, which she'd hauled off from the château by the jarful.

'We found him changed right away, as soon as the girl settled into the house. He began strolling in the park like a big sick bumblebee drawn to the only flower around. He'd walk in circles, in rain and snow and the fiercest wind. Mind you, he'd hardly ever stuck a toe outside before. When he came back from V he would shut himself in his office or in the library. I would bring him a glass of water on a tray — never anything else — and then he would dine at seven o'clock sharp. That was his day, without fail.

'When the teacher moved in, things got a bit irregular. He would come back earlier from court for his walk in the park. He would sit on the bench for long stretches, reading or looking at the trees. And often I might find him at the window, staring out at nothing like an old woman. But his loss of appetite, that was the most alarming. He'd never been a big eater, but now he hardly touched a thing before waving his hand at me to come take it all away. You know, you can't live just on water and air! One of these days, I said to myself, we'll find him on the floor, in his bedroom or somewhere else!

'Thank goodness it never happened. His face just got more and more drawn, especially his cheeks, and his lips, which were hardly there to begin with, got even thinner, like two loose threads. Everything changed. He'd always been early to bed. Now throughout the night I would hear footsteps, slow footsteps from the upper floors, then long silences, only for the slow steps to begin again. I have no idea what on earth he could've been doing — brooding, dreaming, who knows?

'On Sundays he would always manage to cross the girl's path as she was going out. It was always as if by chance, but I saw him not a few times, waiting like a patient cat to pounce. As for her, if she understood what was going on, she certainly didn't let on. She would give him a big hello, clear and hearty, and then be on her way. He would answer, but almost under his breath, with his voice pathetically trailing after her. And of course when she was gone he'd stand there pondering endlessly, as if it were the scene of a crime and he was looking for — who knows what? — a clue maybe, before he'd give up and come inside.'

★ ★ ★

Barbe seemed to relish chatting about the prosecutor and Lysia Verhareine. Anyway, she went on a good long while. The evening was falling around us, with its noises of animals being stabled and shutters banged shut. I imagined the prosecutor walking the paths of the park, heading for the waters of the Guerlante, scanning the windows of the little house where the young teacher lived. That a man who was so near the end of his days should get his feet caught in the nets of love was nothing new. That story's as old as the world. In such cases, all the proprieties go out the window. The absurdity is evident only to others, who just don't understand. Even

Destinat, with his face of marble and his hands of ice, had fallen prey to the unexpected appearance of beauty and the uncontrollable pounding of the heart. In the end, I suppose, that quite simply had made him human.

Barbe said that one evening there had been a grand repast. Destinat had bidden her to get out all the silver, to press the linen napkins and embroidered tablecloths perfectly. Fifty guests? No. Just the young teacher and himself. The two of them alone, at either end of the enormous table. It wasn't Barbe who did the cooking, it was Bourrache, summoned specially from the Rébillon; and Morning Glory served them at table, as Barbe sat brooding by the pantry. Solemn, recognising his uselessness, had trundled off to bed long before. The meal went on till midnight. Barbe strained to discover what on earth they were talking about; she needn't have. Morning Glory told her. 'They're just looking at each other; all they do is look.' Barbe had learned nothing. She began knocking back little glasses of brandy with Bourrache, who ended up waking her towards morning, her head on the kitchen table. At least Bourrache had done all the tidying up, put everything away. He left carrying his daughter in his arms, wrapped in a blanket, sleeping like a baby.

As the night was sidling up to us, the old servant fell silent. She covered her hair with her scarf. The two of us lingered there in the dark for quite a while, saying nothing. Then, suddenly remembering, she dug into the pockets of her old pinafore. Shooting stars cut through the sky, aimless and grotesque — fodder for omens, for those who need them — and then everything was quiet. What shone kept shining; what was dark grew even darker.

'Here,' Barbe said. 'Maybe you'll know what to do with this.'

She handed me a large key.

'Nothing's changed since I stopped going there. His only heir is a distant cousin of his wife's, so distant that we've never seen him. The lawyer says he left for America. I'd be surprised if he ever came back, and it would take forever to track him down. As for me, I won't be around much longer . . . so you'd be the caretaker, in a way.'

Barbe got up slowly, closed my hand around the key, and then went back into her house, without another word. I put the key to the château in my pocket and headed off.

I never had another occasion to speak with Barbe. Even so, the urge came over me often, a bit like a case of scabies that hasn't entirely healed, a strangely pleasant feeling even though it itches. But I told myself I still had time. That's why people are so full of bull; we're always telling ourselves there's plenty of time — we'll be able to do this or that tomorrow, three days from now, next year, in two hours — but then everything dies. We find ourselves following coffins.

I looked at Barbe's the day of her burial as though I could find some answers there, but it was nothing more than well-buffed wood, around which the priest was wafting Latin and puffs of incense. On the way to the cemetery with the meagre, bleating flock, I even wondered whether she hadn't been pulling my leg, that Barbe, with her tales of grand meals and Destinat playing the lover. But in the end it didn't matter. The brandied cherries had sealed her fate. Maybe she was going to find whole cases of them up there, between two clouds.

I still had the key in my pocket, ever since the evening six months earlier when she'd given it to me, though I'd never used it. The shovelfuls of earth put me back on track. The grave was soon filled, and Barbe was reunited with her Solemn, for a heap of eternity. The priest went off with his two choirboys, their little country clogs clacking in the mud. His flock dispersed like starlings in a field of green wheat. As for me, I visited Clémence's grave, kicking myself a bit for not going more often.

The sun, the rain, and the years have all but effaced the photograph I had mounted on her tombstone, in a porcelain medallion. All that remains is the shadow of her hair. I can also make out the outline of her smile, as if she were gazing at me through a veil of gauze. I rested my hand on the gilded letters of her name, and after a while I departed, having told her in my head all these tales of my life — the life I've led without her for all these years. She must know them by heart now; I've trotted them out often enough.

It was on that day, after Barbe's burial, that I made up my mind to go to the château, to delve a bit further, you might say, into the mystery of which I was now one of the few surviving witnesses. Yes, that was the day I pulled aside the rough beard of brambles that hung over the door and slipped the key into the massive lock. I imagined myself a sort of shabby prince, forcing his way over the threshold into the palace of some Sleeping Beauty — except that, on the other side of this threshold, nothing really slept any longer.

9

I still have something I want to say before telling about the château, and its shadows and dust. I want to speak of Lysia Verhareine, since I used to see her too, as everyone else did; our town is small enough that paths always end up crossing. Each time I would raise my hat; and she would return the greeting by lowering her head a bit, with a smile. All the same, one day I saw something else in her eyes, something sharp and cutting; something like a hail of bullets.

It was a Sunday, in the beautiful hours of early evening, in the spring of 1915. The air smelled of apple blossoms and acacia tips. I knew that on Sundays the little teacher always took the same walk that led her to the top of the hill, whether the weather was fair or foul — even if it was raining buckets. At least, so I had heard.

I also used to ramble up there fairly often with a light rifle Edmond Gachentard had passed on to me; he was an old colleague who'd retired from the force to plant cabbages in the Caux region and take care of a crumpled woman in a wheelchair. That rifle is pretty as a lady's jewellery, with a single barrel gleaming like a twenty-sou coin and a butt of cherry wood. On it, Gachentard had had a phrase engraved in slanted script: *You will not feel a thing*. The phrase was addressed to wild game, but Gachentard feared he might take the gun to his wife's head one evening, when the sadness of seeing her like that, with her lifeless legs and ashen face, got to be too much for him. 'I'd rather give it to you,' he'd said, handing it to me wrapped in newspaper — the front page had a picture of the queen of Sweden, I recall. 'Do with it what you like,' he said.

I was amused by the invitation. How much can you do with a rifle, after all? Plant chicory, play music on it, darn your socks, take it to a dance? A rifle is for killing, full stop. I've never had much sympathy for bloodlust but I took the weapon anyway, telling myself that if I left it with Edmond I might come to have a far-off little murder, fuelled by hard cider, on my conscience. Since then I've got into the habit of taking the rifle with me on my Sunday strolls, using it almost as a walking stick. Perhaps his suggestion was not so absurd after all. Over the years the barrel has lost its gleam and taken on a sombre hue that suits it pretty well. The motto engraved by Gachentard has, for lack of proper care, more or less disappeared. Just a few words are still legible — 'not . . . a *thing*' — and true enough, the rifle in my hands has never been used to kill.

Edmond Gachentard had big feet, a Basque beret, and a distressing taste for complicated aperitifs flavoured with plant essences that made them seem disagreeably close to medicinal preparations. He often shook his head while looking at the sky, and would become suddenly meditative whenever large round clouds intruded on a pure blue. 'The bastards,' he would say, but I never really knew whether that applied to the clouds or to some other figures, faraway and shrouded, sailing forth, so to speak, for him alone. There you are; that's all that comes to mind when I think of him. Memory is odd. It retains things not worth three sous. All the rest goes to the grave with us. Gachentard must be dead by now; he'd be a hundred and five years old. His middle name was Marie. Another detail. I'll leave it there.

When I say I'll leave it there, that's really what I ought to do. What good does writing this do, these lines serried like geese in winter, these words I string along with no apparent point? The days pass, and I return to my table. I can't say I enjoy it, but then I can't say I dislike it either.

Yesterday Berthe, who comes to rearrange the dust three times a week, came across one of the notebooks — the first volume, I believe. 'Fine thing, wasting paper like that!' I looked at her. She's stupid, but no more than most. She didn't wait for a response but went on with her housework, singing silly tunes that have been going through her head ever since she was twenty years old and couldn't find a husband. I would have liked to explain a thing or two to her — but explain what? That I move along those lines as on the roads of some unknown and yet familiar country? What's the use? I thought. And when she left, I went back to work. The worst of it is, I don't care what becomes of the notebooks. I'm on number four. I can no longer find two or three. I must have lost them, or perhaps Berthe took them one day to light her stove. It doesn't matter. I don't want to reread. I write, nothing more. It's a bit like talking to myself, a conversation from another time. I lay away portraits. I dig up graves without dirtying my hands.

On that notable Sunday, I had walked for hours along the hill. A little further down lay the town, heaped on itself, house against house — the piled-up mass of the factory buildings in the background, their brick chimneys gouging the sky. A landscape of smoke and work, a sort of shell inhabited by lots of snails without a care for the rest of the world. And yet the world wasn't far off: To see it, all you had to do was climb the hill. That explains no doubt why families preferred to take their Sunday stroll along the banks of the canal, with its genteel melancholy, its calm waters stirred ever so slightly from time to time by the wriggling of a big carp or the prow of a barge. For us, the hill served as a stage curtain, but nobody felt like going to the show. People keep what cowardice they can afford. But for the hill, we would have had the war right in our faces, an honest-to-goodness fact. By the grace of the hill we managed to dodge it, despite the smells and noises it threw our way like so many farts from a sick body. The war mounted its stylish performances behind the hill, on the other side, in a world that wasn't even ours — in other words, nowhere. We refused to be its audience. We made of the war the stuff of legend, and so we were able to live with it.

That Sunday I had climbed higher than usual — oh, not much higher, twenty or thirty metres, somewhat inadvertently — and all on account of a thrush I was following step by step, as it fluttered and chirped, dragging a broken wing beaded with several drops of

75

blood. Since it was the only thing in the world I was focused on, I ended up by reaching the crest, which is a crest in name only, since a great meadow there gives you the impression that an immense hand, its palm held skyward and covered with grasses and low copses, crowns the hill. I felt by the wind in my collar — a warm wind — that I had passed the line, the invisible one that we below have all traced on the earth and in our minds. I raised my eyes, and I saw her.

She was seated casually on the thick grass dotted with daisies, and the pale fabric of her dress scattered around her waist reminded me of the *déjeuners* of certain painters. The pasture and the flowers adorning it seemed to have been arranged for her alone. From time to time the breeze lifted the wispy curls that lent the nape of her neck a soft shadow. She was looking straight ahead, at what the rest of us never wanted to see; she gazed with a beautiful smile, a smile to make the ones she offered us each day — and God knows they were beautiful — seem wan and remote. She looked at the broad plain, dark and infinite, trembling under the far-off vapours of the furious explosions that came to us deadened and decanted — in a word, *unreal*.

There where the front line merged with the horizon — so that at times you might have supposed several suns were rising at once, only to fall back again with the thump of a dud shell — the war unfurled its manly little carnival over many kilometres; from where we were you might have thought it was a miniature scale model of battle. Everything was so small. Death couldn't abide this smallness; it was fleeing and taking its replica of suffering with it — its kit of dismembered bodies, of lost cries of hunger and belliesful of fear, of tragedy.

Lysia Verhareine took it all in with her eyes wide open. She was holding on her knees what at first I took to be a book — but when she began writing a few seconds on, I saw it was the little notebook covered in red morocco. She jotted down some words with a tiny pencil that disappeared in her hand, and as she put those words to paper, her lips were pronouncing others, unless they were the same. I felt like a thief, gazing at her this way behind her back.

I was remarking as much to myself when, slowly, she turned her head towards me, leaving her beautiful smile on the distance of the battleground. Like a right dick, I stood there nailed to the ground, not knowing what to say or do. If I had been totally naked, I couldn't have been more embarrassed. I ventured a little nod. She kept on looking at me, and for the first time I saw her face smooth as a lake in winter: the face of a dead woman. I mean the face of a woman dead within herself, as though nothing inside her was coursing or pulsing any longer, as though her blood had gone somewhere else.

That moment seemed endless as a session of methodical torture. Then her eyes travelled from my face to my left hand, where Gachentard's rifle dangled. I saw what she was seeing. I turned red as a woodpecker's ass. I babbled several words, regretting them immediately. 'It isn't loaded, it's just for — ' And I stopped. I couldn't have sounded any more stupid and in retrospect should have simply held my tongue. She let her eyes linger upon me: a fusillade of darts, acid-tipped, piercing every inch of my skin. Then she shrugged and returned to her landscape, letting me fall back into the universe from which I'd come: a realm much too ugly for her — too narrow, or perhaps too stuffy, of which gods and princesses know nothing, though they sometimes pass through it on tiptoe — the universe of men.

After that Sunday, I put my all into avoiding her whenever I caught sight of her from afar. I sidled through alleys, angled into doorways, or hid under my hat when no other cover was at hand. I could no longer bear to see those eyes, haunted as I was by a great shame, not quite knowing why. What had I seen, after all? A young lady, alone, writing something in a red notebook as she looked out over a landscape of war. I too had a perfect right to be strolling in the orchards if I felt like it!

I hung the rifle on a spike above my door. It's still there. And it has taken the death and burial of everyone for me to begin my Sunday walks again. Since then I've gone up there every time, as on a pilgrimage, to that place in the meadow where I saw the young teacher sitting at the edge of our world.

I always sit in the same place — hers — and catch my breath. That takes quite a few minutes these days. I look out on what she saw, the broad landscape now calm and slow again, without flashes or plumes, and I see her smile once more at the boundless beauty, spattered with desolation. I see all that again as though the scene were to be performed once more, and I wait. I wait.

10

The war went on and on. All those braggarts who were sure we'd be sending the Krauts back home with a quick kick in the arse after three weeks — they shut their traps now. The first anniversary of the hostilities wasn't observed anywhere but at Fermillin's bistro. He was a tall, lanky guy with a head like a candle snuffer who had worked ten years for Northern Railways before discovering his vocation — 'like a call from heaven', he said — for selling spirits.

His place was called Au Bon Pied, the Right Foot. Many had pointed out that the name didn't make much sense for a bar and would confuse the locals. He had replied, curtly enough, that he had reasons of his own for the name he gave his establishment; and as for the townsfolk, they could go to hell.

It didn't take more than a round of drinks on the house for everyone to agree with his logic. Most found that when all was said and done, Au Bon Pied wasn't half bad. It sounded rather distinguished in fact, not so run-of-the-mill as the ubiquitous Excelsior, Floria, Terminus, or Café des Amis. Anyway, the name proved no impediment to business.

On 3 August, 1915, Fermillin unfurled over his sign a big banner made from an old sheet. On it he had written in large red, white, and blue letters: ONE YEAR ON: GLORY TO OUR HEROES!

The party began about five in the afternoon with the faithful: old man Voret, a paunchy retiree from the factory who'd been celebrating his widowhood for three years; Janesh Hiredek, a Bulgarian émigré who spoke French badly when sober but who quoted Voltaire and Lamartine as soon as he had two litres of wine in him; Léon Pantonin, called Green Face, the hue his skin had taken on as a result of a revolutionary treatment for pulmonary inflammation based on copper oxide; Jules Arbonfel, an apelike giant two metres tall but with a girl's voice; and Victor Durel, whose wife would come looking for him at the Bon Pied, only to leave with him two or three hours later, when she had to be carried out herself.

It was going on three in the morning, and the bistro was still resounding with all the old classics: 'Happy, We Depart', 'Madelon', 'The Young Recruits', 'Soldier Boy, My Brother!' The crowd would strike up the choruses and repeat them, practically choking on their own maudlin tears and flowery tremolos. From time to time, the sound of the singing could be heard more clearly as the door swung open to let a combatant out to take a leak under the stars before returning to the belly of the boozy beast. In the morning, you could still hear the groans coming from the joint. There was also the unmistakable odour of stale wine, puke, dirty shirts, and cheap tobacco. Most had spent the night there, sleeping it off. Fermillin, the first to rise, woke the rest as you might shake a plum tree, before selling them breakfast with white pinot.

Lysia Verhareine passed by the café that morning, favouring Fermillin with a smile, which he repaid with a courteous bow and a 'Mademoiselle'. I saw her, but she didn't see me; I was too far off. She wore a dress the ruddy colour of vineyard peaches and a little straw hat adorned with a carmine ribbon. She carried a wide woven handbag, which swung against her hip with a sweet gaiety. She was headed towards the fields. It was August 4. The sun was rising like a flaming arrow and already drying the dew. It would be hot enough to tan the soft skin of desires into leather. You couldn't hear the big guns. Even pricking your ears, you couldn't hear them. Lysia turned the corner at the Mureaux farm and entered the countryside, where the scent of fresh-cut hay and ripened wheat made the earth seem like a huge body, languid with odours and caresses. Fermillin had remained on the threshold of his bistro, his red eyes taking in the sky as he stroked his beard. Youngsters were setting out to roam the world, their pockets stuffed with the simplest of meals. On the clotheslines, women hung out sheets to billow dry in the wind. Lysia Verhareine had disappeared. I imagined her walking down the summer trails as on pathways of sand.

I never saw her again.

I mean, I never saw her alive again. That very evening, Marivelle's son ran to my house and found me naked to the waist, my head drenched in water, dousing myself with a pitcher. When I wiped the water from my eyes, I could see his own were full of fat tears, which poured down his teenage face like dripping wax.

'Come quick, come quick!' he told me. 'Barbe sent me! You've got to come to the château now!'

I knew the way, of course. I left the kid behind and took off like a wild rabbit, imagining I'd discover Destinat disembowelled, probably by an unhappy convict who'd returned, after twenty years' hard labour under the hot sun, to pay his respects. I was even already telling myself on the path to the door that, when all was said and done, he deserved an end like that, the astonished victim of a really savage murder, since among all those heads he'd had over the years there were surely some perfectly innocent ones, people conveyed to the scaffold with their arms and feet firmly bound, screaming for someone to listen to reason.

I arrive at the gate with my hair still wet, my shirt in disarray, my trousers half buttoned, and my heart knocking against my ribs. I see him standing on the flight of steps, ramrod straight, a devilish commander, a true master of morose ceremonies, Swiss Guard of an unholy see: Mr Prosecutor, very much alive, his guts apparently intact and no sign of mayhem on his person. As soon as I see him like that, erect as a flagpole, hands open on nothing, looking off in an awkward daze, I tell myself, If it isn't him; I tell myself — and everything stops. I see Lysia Verhareine, again turning the corner of the Mureaux farm, I see the scene countless times in rapid succession, more real than life itself in all its precise details: the swaying of her dress and her little bag, the nape of her neck white under the rising sun, Bouzie pounding on the anvil in his forge a few steps away, Fermillin's red eyes, old lady Sèchepart whisking a broom in front of her doorstep, the scent of fresh straw, the plaintive cries of the swifts that skim the roofs, the mooing of the cows that Dourin's son is leading to the park. All that, ten times, a hundred times, as though I were taking refuge in this scene, as though I wanted to lock myself inside it forever.

I don't know how many minutes the prosecutor and I faced each other wordless on the steps. I don't much remember our gestures or expressions at that time, anything that could have distinguished one part of that moment from another. It isn't my present memory that's at fault, it's the memory of that moment which, even as it was happening, cut itself to pieces, leaving gaping holes in the fabric of my recollections. Maybe I became an automaton, following him about mechanically; maybe he guided me, took me by the hand. Who knows! My first clear memory is the pounding of my heart I felt once again, the blood in my chest. My eyes were open. The prosecutor was at my left, leading me from behind. The walls of the little tenant house were covered in light-coloured cloth in that room adorned with bouquets of flowers. I recall a few pieces of furniture: a chest of drawers, a wardrobe, a bed.

On her bed lay Lysia Verhareine, her eyes closed. Closed for all time, on the world and on the rest of us. Her hands were clasped upon her chest. She was wearing her dress of that morning, the shade of vineyard peaches, and little shoes of a singular brown — the brown that earth turns when crackled by the sun, when it becomes silky dust. Above her a moth whirred around like a madman, bumping against the half-open window-pane before heading back in precarious circles towards her face, then back again to the window, a dance that seemed like some hideous pavane.

The collar of her dress, slightly open, revealed on the skin of her throat a deep furrow, an almost blackened red. With a feint at the ceiling, the prosecutor indicated a suspended lamp made of blue porcelain, complicated and flanked by a counterweight in the form of a globe — the five continents, the seas and oceans in gleaming copper. Then he drew from his pocket a delicate belt of woven leather, embroidered with daisies and mimosas, out of which a hand, once supple and sweet, had fashioned a loop, the philosopher's very image of perfection, the union of promise and fulfilment, beginning and end, birth and death.

Not a word was said. Our eyes would seek each other's gaze, then return once again to the young teacher's body. Death had not stolen her beauty — not yet, in any case. To that extent, she remained among us, so to speak, the face of a woman almost alive, her complexion very fair. Her hands were still warm when I placed my hand on them, somewhat embarrassed at first, because I expected her to open her eyes, to look at me and protest this intimacy I was presuming. I closed the collar of her dress to hide the finely traced bruise. Now the illusion would be perfect: a sleep that does not speak its true name.

The prosecutor let me be. He didn't dare make a gesture or take a step, and when I turned away from Lysia's face to look at his, I saw in his disoriented eyes a question to which I had no answer. Goddamn it, do I know why people die? Why they choose to die? Do I know any more today than I did then? After all, death was more his game than mine! He was the one who summoned it regularly, knew it on chummy terms, so to speak: an acquaintance he renewed several times a year when he went to the prison yard at V to see his will done before setting off without a qualm to have his lunch at Bourrache's.

I offer him the thin belt, by way of asking if he'd been the one who had . . .

'Yes,' he replied, without my having to

pronounce the word.

I cleared my throat. 'You didn't find anything . . . ?'

He looked around him slowly, at the wardrobe, the chair, the chest of drawers, the dressing table, the bouquets of floral sentinels posted more or less everywhere in the room, the hot thick night forcing the window, the bed, the little curtain, the night table on which sat a delicate watch whose spreading hands continued to move time forward; then he met my eyes once more. 'Not a thing,' he said, still dazed, no longer the prosecutor. I had no way of knowing exactly whether this was a statement or, in fact, another question — or just the words of a man under whom the ground kept giving way.

On the stairway there were the slow, difficult, painful steps of several people: Barbe and Solemn, followed by Hippolyte Lucy, the doctor. A good doctor, thin as a rail, humane and very poor; those two things went hand in hand. If the patient was needy, he hardly ever charged for a house call, and the needy included nearly everyone in our town. 'You can pay me later,' he'd always say, with the most earnest of smiles. 'I'm not hard up,' he'd add with a growl, yet it was poverty that killed him, in 1927. 'Starved to death!' said Desharet, his fat twat of a colleague, with his garlic breath and ruddy face, who'd come from V in an automobile wrapped in chrome, oily leather, and brass to examine the doctor's brittle body. He'd finally been found on the floor in his kitchen — his kitchen unfurnished, without so much as a crust of bread or a pat of butter in sight, only a plate that had been clean for days and a glass of water from the well. 'Starved to death,' the bastard repeated, as though put out by having to bend down to meet the body, over which his belly and jowls were hanging, all trussed up in flannel and English cloth.

Dr Lucy put his hand on the girl's forehead and let it slide down her cheeks, towards the insult on her throat; as soon as he saw it he stopped. He joined our perplexed company, starting his own contemplation of all our questions that would never be uttered. Barbe gave us to understand we had nothing further to do there, in this girl's room, which would remain just that. With a nod, she directed us to the door. We obeyed like children — Solemn, the doctor, the prosecutor, and I.

11

And still the war went on. It had produced so
many bodies there was no point in counting
any more. But the news of the young
teacher's death — and the way it happened
— came as a blow to our town all the same.
The streets were deserted. The gossips, the
fucking backbiters, the old blabbermouths
usually ready with an insinuation, stayed
mum in their houses. The guys in the cafés
just drank in silence. All you heard was the
sound of bottles and swallowing, of glasses
being emptied, nothing more. A stuporous
tribute of sorts. Even the summer seemed to
flag. There were grey, stifling days, as if the
sun didn't dare show its face, spending its
hours behind ample clouds the colour of
mourning. The youngsters weren't hanging
around, or going fishing, or throwing rocks
through windows. Even the livestock seemed
listless. The bells chopped time like a dead
tree trunk. Sometimes the howl of wolves
could be heard, but it was only Martial
Maire, the simpleton who'd understood
everything and who huddled against the door
of the school, bellowing. Maybe all of us

should have done likewise. Maybe there's nothing else you can do in such circumstances.

I should have asked the prosecutor some questions. That's the way it's done in cases of violent death — of suicide, I mean, since we have to call a spade a spade. Yes, I should have. It was my duty, but I let it go. Could he have added anything to what I knew? Not much, I'll wager. And facing him I would have felt like a prick, twisting my cap, looking at the floor, the ceiling, my hands, without daring to come to the point — whatever that was. He was the one who'd found her. He was taking a stroll when he'd noticed the open window and seen the body. He'd rushed over, forced the door of the room — locked from the inside — and then . . . nothing more. He took her in his arms and laid her on the bed. Then he sent for me. All that he told me, once Barbe had led us out and we walked around on the lawn without knowing where to go or what to do.

★   ★   ★

In the days that followed, Destinat remained secluded in his château. He spent his hours at a window, looking at the little house as though expecting the young teacher to appear. This much I would learn from the evening of Barbe's brandied testimony.

We tried to find out whether Lysia Verhareine had a family — or, rather, I tried a bit and the mayor tried very hard. We came up empty-handed. Just an address on some envelopes, a crossed-out address of a former landlady; the mayor spoke with her on the telephone but only half understood her because of her northern accent. All the same, he grasped that she knew nothing of her former tenant. When letters arrived, the landlady would forward them to the new address — that of the château — which the girl had sent to her. 'And were there a lot of letters?' the mayor asked, with me right there next to him. He never got an answer. The telephone cut off. In those days it was still unreliable. And it was wartime besides. Even the telephone had been mobilised, I guess.

Next we questioned Marcel Crouche, the mailman, who never managed to finish his rounds because of other rounds he never refused: rounds of wine, brandy, coffee with rum, Pernod, and vermouth. By late morning, he would end up sitting against the wall of the washhouse, slurring political humbug and then snoring like a saw, his mailbag clutched under his arm. With the château towards the end of his route, he was by then already walking as if on the bridge of a ship, tossed by a heavy storm.

'Letters — sure there were letters. I looked at the address, not the name. When it said château, it was for the château. Whether it was for the prosecutor or the young lady, I know fuck-all. I just delivered them, and he sorted it out. I always give mail to the prosecutor himself, never to Barbe or to Solemn. That's how he wants it, and after all it's his house.'

Marcel Crouche poked his big nose, ravaged by smallpox, into his glass of brandy, sniffing the liquid like the very elixir of life, which I suppose for him it was. All three of us drank in silence, the mayor, the mailman, and me. Then there was another round. From the expressions on our faces, the mayor and I figured we were thinking the same thing. But we also both knew that neither one of us would dare put the question to the prosecutor. So we didn't speak of it.

At the Public Education Bureau, they didn't know much more, only that Lysia Verhareine had volunteered for a post in the region. The inspector, whom I'd made a special trip to V to see, made me wait three-quarters of an hour in his hallway, just to make sure I knew what an important man I was calling on. He seemed less concerned

93

about the teacher than about his right moustache, which he couldn't smooth down despite ample pomade. He butchered her name several times, made like he was hunting through the files, consulted his lovely gold watch, patted his hair down, studied his spotless nails. He had the eyes of a calf, the sort of fucking dumb animals that don't even moan when you lead them off to their death, because they never even suspect that such a mystery exists. He called me 'my dear fellow', but in his mouth it sounded like something that had formed in the back of his throat that he was trying to clear out.

After a while he rang for a minion, but nobody answered. Then he shouted. Still no answer. He started howling, and a sickly head resembling a dried-out turnip appeared. The head coughed every thirty seconds, a cough that came from very far away to announce that all good things must end, the body no exception. The turnip head was called Mazerulles. The inspector spat out his name like a whiplash, asking him to rack his brain. He did remember the girl, the day she'd arrived.

People don't always look the part. You would have thought this scarecrow was just a dumbbell bureaucrat, somebody's soulless doormat, good for nothing else. But when I started talking about the girl, and I told him what had happened, it was as if I'd nailed him between the eyes with a plank. He braced himself on the doorframe, stammering disjointed sentiments about youth, beauty, waste, war, the end. It was just the two of us now, Mazerulles and me, with a little ghost that came to commune with us, phrase by phrase.

The inspector sensed this, the clod; he began to stamp his feet, breathing hard and repeating 'Good. Very good. Very good,' as though his patience for this matter had run out. I left the office in the company of Mazerulles, without saying goodbye to the stuffed shirt, who stank of starch and department-store cologne. The door slammed shut behind us. We went into the secretary's office: tiny, sad, and rickety, not unlike its occupant. It smelled of wet cloth and firewood, also of menthol and coarse tobacco. He offered me a chair near the stove and sat down behind his little table with three plump inkwells.

Shaking off his astonishment, he recounted Lysia Verhareine's visit. His story was straightforward and it wasn't any help, but I enjoyed hearing her talked about by someone else, someone not from our town. It was proof I wasn't dreaming, that she'd really existed, this guy I didn't know from Adam summoning her in front of me. On my way out I shook Mazerulles's hand and wished him good luck; I don't know why, it just slipped out. He didn't seem surprised. He said to me simply, 'My luck, you know . . . ' I didn't know, but looking at him I could imagine.

Now what should I say? I could describe Lysia Verhareine's burial. It was on Monday. The weather was as beautiful as the day she'd chosen to take her leave of us, maybe even warmer. Yes, I could tell about all that: the sun, the children who'd woven garlands of grapevines and wheat, every last inhabitant crowded into the church, which seemed it might burst, Bourrache and his little girls, the prosecutor in the first pew like a widower, and the fat priest, Father Lurant, newly arrived, whom we'd distrusted until then but who found some very apt words to express what many of us had in our hearts — a priest who could truly make the funeral seem something only natural. I could tell about all that, but I haven't the heart.

Actually, it was the prosecutor who was most changed. He kept on asking for a head now and then, but it seemed his heart was no longer in it. Worse, he sometimes muddled up his closing arguments. Well, that's not completely accurate. It would be better to say that sometimes, in the course of reiterating the facts and drawing his conclusions, he would slow down, stare into space, and just stop talking. As though he weren't there any longer, in his speaker's chair at the courthouse. As though he were absent. It would never last very long, never to the point where someone might have thought of tugging at his sleeve to get him started again; but there was a certain embarrassment, and when he resumed his closing argument, everybody seemed relieved, even the guy on trial.

The prosecutor had the little house in the park bolted up. There was never another tenant there, just as there wouldn't be another teacher at the school until the end of the war. Destinat stopped strolling in the park as well. He went out less and less. We learned somewhat later that it was he who had paid for the coffin and the monument. We all considered this a handsome gesture on his part.

A few months after the teacher's death, I learned from Léon Schirer, a guy who served as a kind of handyman at the court-house in V, that Destinat had requested retirement. Schirer wasn't one for idle talk, but I could hardly believe him. For one thing the prosecutor, though no longer young, still had some good years ahead of him. More than that, I couldn't imagine what he could possibly do with himself, alone in a house big enough for a hundred, with two servants he barely said three words to on any given day.

But I was wrong. Destinat delivered his last closing argument on 15 June, 1916. He delivered it without believing it. And in fact he didn't get the defendant's head. Once the courtroom emptied out, the president made a speech, sober and short, and then a sort of aperitif was served, with the whole bench — headed up by Mierck — lawyers, court clerks, and some others. I was there too. Nearly everyone went to the Rébillon for a farewell meal. I say *nearly*. For myself, I wasn't there. For some sparkling wine, they could suffer my presence; but for the truly good things — things meant to be savoured by those born to them — as far as they were concerned, I could go back where I came from.

After that, Destinat entered into silence.

12

To continue, I must go back to the December morning of 1917 when I left the little body of Morning Glory at the edge of the freezing canal, along with Judge Mierck and his shivering entourage.

All this must seem a muddle, back and forth in time, but in fact it's the very image of my life, made of nothing but jagged bits and pieces, impossible to stick back together. If you would try to understand a human being, you have to dig down to the roots. It's not enough to nudge him along through time, into a flattering light: You have to probe the cracks and let all the poison seep out. You need, in other words, to get your hands dirty. But nothing disgusts me, it's my job. Besides, it's dark outside. What else could I do at night but get out the same old sheets and mend them a little more, and a little more?

Mierck still had egg yolk stuck to his moustache and his haughty air of a gouty ambassador. His delight at the proximity of the château to this scene of death lingered in the corners of his mouth. The little door that led into the park was open, and the grass was trodden here and there. The judge started to whistle and swing his cane seat, as though it were a fly whisk. The sun had now pierced the fog and was making the frost drip. We were stiff, our cheeks as hard as wooden soles. Crusty had stopped taking notes — notes on what anyway? Everything had been said. 'Well, well, well,' Mierck continued, rocking on his heels.

Then he turned quite suddenly to the city policeman. 'Give him my compliments!'

The other man was taken aback. 'Who do you mean, Judge?'

Mierck looked at him as though he had a bean where his brain should be. 'Who? Why, the person who cooked the eggs, my friend. They were excellent. Where is your head? Get a grip on yourself!' The city policeman saluted. The judge used to address people as 'my friend' in a tone that implied he considered them nothing of the sort. He had a knack for using words to say things they normally didn't mean.

We could have lingered there a good while longer: the judge, the policeman (exemplary fetcher of eggs), Crusty, Bréchut's son, Grosspeil, Berfuche and myself. The judge hadn't said a word to me; it was always like that. The doctor, with his leather bag and his kid gloves, had taken off a while before. He had left Morning Glory — or rather the outward form of a little girl's body — under the wet blanket. The canal continued reeling out its swift waters. I then remembered a Greek saying, without recalling it too well, one that spoke about time and running water, some simple words that said everything about life. Above all, they made you understand you could never go back, no matter how hard you try.

Two ambulance orderlies finally arrived, biting their lips, freezing in their thin white smocks. They'd come from V and driven around a long time before finding the place. The judge beckoned to them, pointing at the blanket. 'It's all yours!' he called out, as if it were some old piece of furniture he had sold them. It was then I left, without a word to anyone.

Of course, I was obliged to come back to the waterside. I had to do my job, to say nothing of the duty of being human, which isn't all that easy. I waited till early afternoon. The sharp bite of the morning had relaxed; the weather was almost mild. It seemed like another day entirely. Grosspeil and Berfuche had been relieved by two other policemen guarding the scene and fending off the gawkers. As they saluted me, some carp slipped between the algae. Now and then one of them rose to the surface to test the air before swimming off with a swish of the tail to take its place again in the little school. The grass shimmered with countless drops of water. Everything had already changed. You could no longer discern the outline that Morning Glory's body had impressed on the bank. Two ducks were fighting over a watercress cushion. One of them ended up snapping at the other's neck; the loser went off, scattering plaintive cries in his wake.

I dawdled a while, trying to look for clues but unable to think of much except Clémence and the baby in her womb. In fact I felt a bit ashamed, as I recall, to think of them and our happiness when I was walking near the place where someone had killed a little girl. I knew I would be seeing them again in just a few hours: her and her belly, round as a prize pumpkin, through whose shell I could hear the heartbeat and feel the sleepy movements when I put my ear against it. Without a doubt, on this icy day I was the happiest man on earth, the same earth on which, not far from here, men were killing and dying as freely as we draw breath; on which, right beneath my feet, a murderer without a face could strangle little ewe lambs ten years old. Yes, the happiest of men, without a shred of guilt about it.

The strange thing about the inquiry was that it got assigned to everybody and nobody. Mierck made a mess of it. The mayor stuck his nose in. The policemen sniffed the pile of shit from a distance. But taking the lead was a colonel who showed up the day after the crime and used the state of war and our being in the front-line zone as an excuse to claim authority to give us orders. He was called Matziev, a vaguely Russian name. Elegant, he looked like a Neapolitan dancer, with an oily voice, a glossy head of hair he kept brushed back, a thin moustache, supple legs, and the torso of a Greek wrestler. In short, an Apollo with rank.

We sized him up right away. He had a taste for blood but, being on the right side, he could make it flow and drink it without giving offence. The hotel having closed for lack of guests, he set up quarters at the home of Bassepin, who rented out a few rooms and sold charcoal, oil, grease, and canned beef to all the regiments that passed through.

The war years were the best of Bassepin's life. Selling exorbitantly what he'd gone far away for and bought for peanuts. Stuffing his pockets, working day and night, palming off the essential and the superfluous alike on the quartermasters who came through, at times taking back what he'd sold to regiments now departing so he could pass it on to the ones relieving them. A typical commerce-made man.

The post-war years weren't so unpleasant for him either. Very quickly, he understood the municipal frenzy to honour those who had died in combat. Bassepin expanded his business and sold cast-iron soldier boys and French cockerels by the ton. All the mayors of the eastern region snapped up his rigid warriors, with flags in the air and rifles aimed; he had them designed by a tubercular painter, an 'award-winner in the exhibitions'. They came in any price range, suitable for all budgets: twenty-three models in the catalogue, with options ranging from marble pedestals and gold lettering to obelisks. There were little tin children holding out laurels to the victors and allegories of France as nubile goddess, her breast bare and comforting. Bassepin was selling memory and memento. The cities settled their debts with the dead in a very visible way, one that would last. On every November 11, before those monuments surrounded by gravel walks and linden trees, a full-throttled brass band would blast out the lively airs of triumph and the bleary ones of pain, while at night stray dogs would lift their legs all around and pigeons would add their decorations to those bestowed by men.

Bassepin had a big pear-shaped belly and sported a moleskin cap, winter and summer, a stick of liquorice hanging from his mouth, and black teeth. A fifty-year-old bachelor, he'd never had so much as an affair as far as we knew. The money he had, he kept; he didn't gamble and was never to be seen in the brothels of V. He didn't even take a drink. No indulgence, no appetite, just the mania of buying and selling, of stashing gold away for its own sake. A bit like those who stuff their barns with hay up to the gills when they don't have any animals. But after all, that was his right: to die as rich as Croesus in 1931 of septicaemia. Incredible how a tiny wound can wreck your life and even end it. It started on his foot, just a graze, hardly a scratch. Five days later he was stiff, blue all over, mottled from head to toe, like an African savage covered with paint but without the kinky hair and the assegai. No heir. Not a tear shed by anyone, in fact. It wasn't that people loathed him — far from it. But his preoccupations were known, and they did not invite pity. He had had everything he wished for; not everyone can say the same. Maybe that was the reason for Bassepin's life, to come into this world and collect its coins. In the end it's no stupider than anything else. He made the most of it. On his death, all the money went to the government, a very fair and merry widow.

Bassepin gave Matziev the finest room he had and would raise his moleskin hat to the colonel whenever their paths crossed. It was a rare chance to see — among the three or four hairs duelling for supremacy on his bald pate — a large port-wine stain quite remarkably shaped like the American continent.

Matziev's first important order of business in town was to have his aide find him a gramophone. He could be seen for hours at the window of his room, shutters open despite the unremitting cold, smoking cigars as slender as shoelaces and pausing every five minutes to wind up his crackly companion. He always listened to the same song, a catchy hit tune from several years before, when we all still believed the world was eternal and when to be happy required only our believing we would be:

> Caroline, put on your li'l patent-leather
>   shoes . . .
> Caroline, I'm telling you . . .

Twenty times, a hundred times a day, Caroline put on her adorable shoes while the colonel smoked his little brown stinkers with an elegant air, a limp wrist, and rings on every finger, letting his black eyes dally on each surrounding roof. The song still runs through my head today, setting my teeth on edge. It was the theme of our bereavement, our thoughts of Morning Glory and of the face of the beast who had done that unspeakable thing. The colonel had cranked his gramophone like a drill, which slowly made its meticulous hole in our skull, to let the treacly tune seep in. At bottom, this song was the cousin of the judge's eggs, a 'little world' to be savoured, to deliver one from the bleakness of death. No wonder those two, Mierck and Matziev, though different as could be, got on like old friends.

13

Considering what he did — and I'll get to that soon enough — we might put Matziev squarely in that most numerous species of bastards on earth, the one that breeds like rabbits and thrives like roaches. But nothing is simple. Only saints and angels never make mistakes.

He is the same man who in 1894 — twenty-three years before the Case — had scuppered his own career, owing to a much more famous affair, and had languished as a lieutenant for ages while the others earned their stripes in due course. Mind you, he was not a tinsel Dreyfusard or one who spoke up only at the family dinner table; there were thousands of those. No, in those days Matziev had the balls of a bull, and he supported the little captain quite publicly, declaring sincere faith in his innocence. This rearguard action, so to speak, attacking the good judgement of the staff officers, won him no friends in their ranks. With one gesture, he fell from grace in the eyes of all those who would most likely have been content to see a man of his type handsomely promoted and propelled towards the stars — the ones that are sewn on, made of solid gold.

All that is History with a capital H, as they say, but it often falls between the cracks and only gets fished out by accident, while we're rummaging through attics or old heaps of trash.

I happened on it that way: It was in 1926, the year my father died. I had to return to the ramshackle house where I'd been born and raised. I didn't want to hang around. My father was one more dead man, and I'd already had my fill of those for a lifetime. That house was the house of my dead; my mother — God keep her soul — had passed long ago, when I was still a little rascal, and now my father. It was no longer the home of my early years. The house now smelled of the grave.

The village too no longer resembled the one I had known. After four years of endless bombardments, everyone had left, abandoning the gutted buildings and the pitted streets. The only ones to stay were my father — because for him, leaving would have meant victory for the Krauts, despite their defeat — and Fantin Marcoire, an old nutter who talked to trout and lived with a very old cow he called Madame.

Fantin and his cow slept side by side in the

stable. They had ended up resembling each other, as to odour and the rest, except that the cow was undoubtedly more sensible than the man and less aggressive. Fantin detested my father, and the feeling was mutual. They had known each other since their schooldays, and neither could explain the persistent grudge. They had chased the same girls, played the same games — felt the same pains, no doubt — and time had worn them down just as it wears down the bodies and hearts of all men. But not the mutual loathing of those two. And so there they were: two madmen in a ghost town, hurling abuse, and occasionally stones, at each other among the ruins, like two urchins but with wrinkled foreheads and crooked legs. Every morning before dawn, Fantin Marcoire came to pull down his trousers and shit in front of my father's door. And every evening, my father would wait till Fantin Marcoire bedded down against the flank of his cow to do likewise in front of his neighbour's door.

That went on for years, like a ritual form of greeting: the manners of the lower abdomen.

★ ★ ★

'So he's dead?'
'Dead as can be, Mr Marcoire.'

'The son of a bitch, how could he do that!'

'He was on in years.'

'That means I am too, I suppose?'

'That's what it means, Mr Marcoire.'

'The bag of shit, how could he leave me here alone? What am I supposed to do now?'

'You've got to leave, go somewhere else, Mr Marcoire.'

'You've got some bright ideas, haven't you, you little shit. You're a stupid shit like your bloody father, put on earth just to plague me! . . . You think he suffered much?'

'I don't think so.'

'Not even a little?'

'Maybe, I don't know. Who can tell?'

'Me, I'm going to suffer — for sure. I feel like it's already starting, the bastard!'

★   ★   ★

Fantin left by what had been the main street of the village. He avoided the old bombshell craters only by theatrically serpentine detours. Every three metres he cursed the dead. Then he disappeared, after turning the corner at Camille's store, Favours, Notions, and Novelties, its shutters gutted like the shattered keys of a gigantic derelict piano.

My father's house was a pigsty. I tried hard to summon up lost tunes, memories, images

111

of yesteryear, but nothing came to me. Filth and dust had stiffened everything. It was like the large coffin of a fool who thought he could take everything with him but who had lost his nerve in the end. I recalled what the teacher had told us about Egypt, about its pharaohs' tombs crammed with their earthly riches. My father's house was a bit like that, though never having been a pharaoh he had laid away, in the place of gold and jewels, towers of dirty dishes and empty wine bottles, stacked in all the rooms in large piles, wobbly and translucent.

I never loved my father, and I didn't even know why. I never hated him either. We just hadn't spoken much, that's all. My mother's death had come between us early on — a thick muffling curtain. Neither of us had dared to draw it open and hold out a hand to the other.

In what had been my room, he had taken up an entrenched position, a rubbish fort with parapets of old newspapers piled high. Of the window there remained only a thin slit through which he could spy Fantin Marcoire's ramshackle stable. On the floor, there were two slingshots made of hazel wood and inner tubing, such as boys make to shoot at crows and policemen's bums. Next to them, a munitions dump of rusty staples and twisted screws, a bitten piece of sausage, a half-empty bottle of heady wine beside a dirty glass.

From this position my father had waged his war, bombarding the perennial enemy with small bits of scrap iron whenever the latter emerged from his beastly dwelling. I imagined him spending hours there, brooding and drinking, his eyes glued to the slit of light, his ears cocked for sounds from the street. And then suddenly he would load his slingshot, hold his breath, and take aim, not exhaling until he heard the yells, saw Fantin bitterly rubbing his side or his cheek or his arse, maybe wiping away a bit of blood on a good day, before defiantly brandishing a fist and spewing his venomous curses. Thus my father earned the right to slap his thighs and dissolve into side-splitting guffaws, on and on, till the laughter petered out in grotesque hiccups, not a laugh any longer but a mutter. Catching his breath, he'd turn serious again, go back to his boredom, his emptiness. Pouring himself some more wine with a trembling hand, he'd drink it in one gulp, like hard spirits, and then reflect that there's not much to us, no, not much, and even this can't last much longer, even though a day is very long, and you've got to keep going, because there will be other days to take a gulp from the bottle and consider that we're nothing.

On the way out my shoulder unsettled a stack of newspapers, which collapsed with the rustle of withered leaves. Lost days scattered at my feet, dead years, bygone dramas. From among the jumble of headlines that had lost all urgency, one jumped out at me, with Matziev's name in big letters, above a short item from 1894.

It was late in the year, on a December day. Evening, to be precise. Lieutenant Isidore Matziev, it reported,

. . . had proclaimed his belief in the innocence of Captain Dreyfus in the back room of a café. Applauded by the assembly of unionists and revolutionaries, Matziev, in full uniform, also declared his shame at serving in an army that would imprison the just while letting real traitors go unpunished.

The approval of the crowd was interrupted by the arrival of the police. Several arrests were made, including the lieutenant, and a more than sufficient number of blows were dealt with truncheons. Considered a troublemaker for breaking the code of silence and tarnishing the French army's honour, Lieutenant Matziev had appeared two days later before a military tribunal that condemned him (two days prior to this report) to six months of close arrest.

The hack who'd written the piece concluded by huffing about the young officer's insolent manner and his name, which 'smacked of a Jew, or a Russian, unless it was both'. It was signed Amédée Prurion, a nice idiotic name for a real bastard. Whatever became of this Prurion? Did he keep on vomiting his petty bile for years and years? If he's dead today, that makes one less bag of shit on earth. If he's still alive, he can't be a pretty sight. Hate is a cruel marinade; it gives meat a flavour of trash, no doubt about it: though I knew him only as a son of a bitch, Matziev was worth ten Prurions. At least he could point to one time in his life when he hadn't disgraced his humanity. How many can say as much?

I kept the article as proof — of what I don't know. I never went back to the house; life can't stand returns. I remembered the Matziev I had known: his thin waxed moustache, his twisted cigars, his gramophone scratching out the little song. He disappeared eventually, with all his kit, once the Case had been settled — settled for them, you understand. No doubt he'd gone on lugging his 'Caroline' around with him, going

115

through the motions. Whenever our eyes had met, he gave the impression of a man who had reached his destination. Wherever he happened to be, it no longer served any purpose for him to put himself out. All that was behind him. The only thing left for him was to wait for the final rendezvous.

★ ★ ★

The snow fell for hours last night. I kept hearing it as I sought sleep in my bed. Or perhaps it's better to say I was hearing its silence and sensing its pervasive whiteness behind the improperly closed shutters, a whiteness that intensified hour by hour.

All that silence and whiteness, cutting me off still more from the world. Just what I need! Clémence loved this snow. 'If it comes, there couldn't be a more beautiful blanket for our baby.' She would never know the extent of that truth. The beautiful blanket would cover her too.

At seven o'clock I pushed the door open. The landscape was out of a pastry shop: cream and powdered sugar everywhere. I blinked as though before a miracle. The low sky was rolling its heavy humps on the crest of the hill, and the factory, which usually blew its stack with rage, was reduced to purring, almost a pleasant sound. A new world. The first morning of a new world. Like being the first man. Before the stains, the trail of footprints — and of misdeeds. I don't really know how to put it better. Words were never easy for me. I hardly used them when I was still alive. If I write as if I'm a dead man, as a matter of fact, that's true, true as true can be. For a long time I've felt like one, just keeping up a pretence of living for a while longer. I'm serving a suspended sentence, you might say.

My movements betray rheumatism, but they still have a mind of their own. They want to make me go round in circles, like a donkey tied to his millstone, grinding the last grain. To lead me back to feeling. It's their fault I found myself on the bank of the little canal, which traced, in the whiteness, a green net trimmed with melting stars. As I sank into the snow, I thought of Napoleon's bloody retreat across the Berezina River: an epic. Maybe that's what I need to persuade myself there really is some meaning to life, that for all my feeling lost I'm headed in the right direction, straight into the history books, for centuries to come; that maybe Fate had a plan in causing me to postpone my departure so many times, the barrel of Gachentard's rifle pulled away fast at the last moment, not slowly as I had slipped it down my throat, on mornings when I awoke to feeling like a dried-out well. The taste of a rifle — what an odd thing! The prickling in your tongue when it's peeled off the freezing barrel. The flavours, like wine, pale rocks.

Some stone martens had fought a skirmish here. Their claw-studded paws had left calligraphies, arabesques, a madman's testimony on the snow. Their bellies left runs and described shallow paths that diverged and then crossed, melting into each other, and then diverged again before stopping short, as though suddenly, at the end of their little battle, both animals had taken flight.

'So old and so fucking dumb . . . '

I thought the cold was playing tricks on me.

'You want to catch your death?' the voice continued, coming as though from afar, all raspy consonants, clinking medals. No need to turn around. It was Joséphine Maulpas. Born the same year I was, in the same village too. Moved here when she was thirteen years old and went to work as an all-purpose maid. She kept it up till she was twenty, passing from one well-to-do family to another as she cultivated a taste for the bottle, bit by bit — until there was not another family that would have her. Thrown out, chucked, rejected, done for. To survive, she took up the stinking trade of selling animal skins: rabbits, moles, weasels, ferrets, foxes, all sorts, dangling by her side still bloody, freshly stripped with a pocketknife. Thirty years and more of trundling her goitrous cart through the streets, bleating out monotonously, 'Rabbit skins! Animal skins! Rabbit skins!' Most people simply stopped hearing her after a time, as she took on the butchery scent of her carcasses and, before long, their appearance too — their purple complexion, their leaden eyes — she who once had been a real beauty.

For a few coins, Joséphine — dubbed the Skin by the kids in town — sold her prizes to Elphège Crochemort, who tanned them in an abandoned mill on the banks of the Guerlante, six kilometres upstream from us. Half in ruins, the old mill took in water like a big open ship; but it remained standing all the same, season after season.

Crochemort rarely came to town, but when he did you could follow his trail. You could easily tell which street he'd gone down, his stench was so awful, regardless of season or time of day, as if he himself had soaked in those alkali vats. Notwithstanding, he was a tall, rather handsome man, with swept-back shiny black hair and lively eyes of a beautiful azure blue. A very handsome man indeed, and quite alone. I always saw him as one of the perpetually condemned, like the ones they say existed among the Greeks, forever rolling their boulders uphill or getting their livers eaten. Had Crochemort done something awful that haunted him? Maybe he was paying for it with his solitude and smell of carrion, for if he'd only been rubbed with lavender and jasmine, he'd have had all the women at his feet.

Joséphine took him her booty every week. She'd long since been indifferent to the odours and — even before she took up her trade — to men as well. But Elphège Crochemort received her like a queen, or so she told me. He would offer her a glass of wine, speak graciously of the skins, of the fair weather or foul, and smile in a way that showed his fine features to advantage. Then he would pay her and help her unload her cart before escorting her back to the road as a beau might have done.

For twenty years Joséphine had lived at the far end of rue des Chablis, almost in the fields. Not a house, really, just a few planks blackened by the rain, held together thanks to some daily miracle. A shack so dark it scared the kids. We all imagined it was chock-full of stinking hides, dead animals, dismembered birds, and mice with limbs outstretched tacked to little boards.

I did go there, twice. I wouldn't have believed it but for having seen it with my own eyes. It was like passing through the doors of a shadow world and emerging into a realm of light. You would have thought you had entered a doll's rooms, an immaculate place, all in rosy tones with little curls of ribbon tied everywhere.

'So you thought I would live as I work,' Joséphine said to me the first time, as I stood open-mouthed, like a bream at the market, taking it all in. There was a bouquet of irises on a table spread with a lovely cloth; on the walls, painted frames surrounded pictures of cherubs and saints, the kind priests give to altar boys and to children at First Communion.

'You believe in all this?' I asked her, pointing with my chin at the graceful gallery. She shrugged her shoulders, less in mockery than to suggest the obvious: There was hardly any point in discussing the matter.

'If I had beautiful copper pans, I'd hang them up just like that, and they'd create the same effect — the feeling that the world isn't so ugly, that there's a bit of gilding here and there.'

I felt her hand on my shoulder. Then her other hand, and finally the heat trapped in her woollen layers.

'Why've you come back here, Dadais?'

It was the nickname Joséphine had used for me since we were seven years old, but I'd never asked why. I was about to answer, to launch into grandiose sentiments right by the water, standing in my shirtsleeves, my feet in the snow. But the cold made my lips tremble, and suddenly I felt the shock of imagining never being able to leave again.

'You've come back, haven't you?'

'I'm only passing through; it's not the same. There's nothing for me here. I don't have regrets. I did what had to be done. I did my part, and you know it.'

'But I always believed you!'

'You were the only one.'

Joséphine rubbed my shoulders, as if to shake some sense into me. The pain of the blood returning to my veins gave me a tonic jolt. Then she took me by the arm and we ambled along, an odd couple in the snow that winter morning. We walked without saying a word. Now and then I glanced sideways, looking in her ancient face for her former girlish features, a futile effort. I let myself be led around like a child. I would have gladly closed my eyes and somnambulated, placing one foot in front of the other, hoping deep in my heart never to open my eyes again, to go on and on like this in what might have been death or else a slow stroll, without aim or end.

At my house, Joséphine sat me down with authority in the big armchair and wrapped me snugly in three coats, one layered on the other; now I was an infant again. She went off to the kitchen. I put my feet up near the stove. In my body, bit by bit, everything was coming back — the stirs and the aches, the creaks and the cracks. She handed me a boiling-hot bowl of steaming plum brandy and lemon. I drank without saying anything. She drank too. When she finished her bowl, she clicked her tongue regretfully.

'Why didn't you ever get married again?'

'What about you? You've stayed all alone.'

'I knew everything about men by the time I was fifteen. You have no idea what it's like to be a servant! Never again, I said to myself, and I've kept that promise. But you — it's not the same.'

'I still talk to her, you know, every day. There just wasn't room for another woman.'

'Admit it: you've assumed the airs of the prosecutor!'

'Nothing to do with it.'

'Says you. You've been brooding so long, you're even starting to look like him — that's how old couples are.'

'Don't be stupid, Fifine.'

We fell silent for a while, then she picked it up again. 'I saw him that evening, I swear I did, with my own eyes. Even if that other bastard didn't want to believe me — what was his name again, that pig in a suit?'

'Mierck.'

'He's dead, I hope?'

'In 'thirty-one. His horse kicked his head in.'

'Better than he deserved. But what cause could he have had to doubt you? You were the policeman!'

'He was the judge.'

I couldn't keep my mind from rushing through the years once again, ending up at the same point where I always do. Rather like reaching the outskirts of one's region. From here, I know the road too well.

14

Joséphine had come to find me three days after the discovery of Morning Glory's body. The inquiry was leading nowhere. The police were questioning people at random. Matziev was cranking his gramophone, listening to his song. Mierck had returned to V. As for me, I was trying to understand.

Clémence had gone to answer the door, her hands, as always, on her great belly, as one might lay hands on a globe of the earth. She knew Joséphine slightly and let her come in, despite her terrifying appearance and her reputation as a witch.

'Your wife was so gentle.' Joséphine handed me the bowl, now refilled. 'I don't remember her features well, but I do remember that she was gentle, everything about her, her eyes, her voice.'

I said, 'I don't have her face any longer either. I look for it often; I have the impression it's coming to me, but then it fades away. At that moment I could beat myself senseless.'

'What for, stupid?'

'Not remembering the face of the woman I

loved. What kind of bastard does that make me?'

Joséphine shrugged. 'Bastards, saints — can't say I've ever seen one or the other. Souls are never black or white; they're all grey in the end, Dadais. You're a grey soul for sure, just like the rest of us.'

'It's just words, Fifine. They don't change a thing.'

'What have you got against words?'

I had offered her a seat and she'd told me her story at one go, in very specific terms. Clémence had retired to our bedroom. I knew what she was making in there — with needles, lace, balls of blue and pink wool — for weeks already. I thought about her in the room nearby as Joséphine spoke: thought of her fingers flying over the needles, of her belly and those feet kicking hard from inside. And then, bit by bit, as Morning Glory's sodden body entered the room, she came and sat down beside me, as though to listen to what Joséphine had to tell and say yes or no. So bit by bit, I could think of nothing. I was listening to Joséphine. I was seeing Morning Glory — the dead girl's dripping face, her closed eyes, her lips chilled blue. I seemed to see her smile. She nodded her head now and then; her mouth appeared to say, *Yes, it's true, that's right, it's just like the Skin says. Everything happened like that.*

So. On the day before the body was discovered, about six o'clock, she tells me — dusk, the hour of daggers and stolen kisses — Joséphine heads for home, pulling her cart, taking a swig of warmth from a brandy flask always in the pocket of her smock. Strangely, despite the cold, the walking wounded crowd the streets as on red-letter days; all of them out on the town — the amputees, the legless, the broken-faced, the eyeless, the trepanned, the half mad — wandering from bistro to bar, emptying glasses to fill their hearts.

At the outset, after the first battles, it had seemed very odd to us to see these guys who were our own age, coming back with their faces redrawn by shell bursts, their bodies shredded by sudden downpours of bullets, while we led our narrow little lives in warmth and peace.

We weren't unaware of the war. We'd seen the mobilisation posters. We followed it attentively in the papers. But in fact we were miming; we'd come to terms with it, as you do with bad dreams and bitter memories. It really didn't belong to our world. It was something out of the movies.

And so, when the first convoy of wounded — I'm speaking of the truly wounded, those of whom there was nothing left but a reddish pulp and who lay in trucks on flea-infested stretchers, softly groaning and chanting their mother's name or their wife's — when that first convoy showed up in our town, it hit us right between the eyes. Suddenly there was a great silence, and we all came to see them, these shadows of men, when the litter bearers brought them out to carry them into the clinic. Two rows, dense and thick — a row of honour, a row of horror — as the women bit their lips and wept continuously, while the rest of us, mugs at heart, felt shamed. But also — it's awful but it has to be said — we felt happy, an overwhelming and unwholesome joy, that it was them and not us lying there.

All that was in September 1914. This first wave of wounded were spoiled rotten. Endless visits, bottles, pies, madeleines, liqueurs, fine batiste shirts, corduroy trousers, pork treats, stoppered wine.

And then time went to work. Time and toll, because they started arriving every day by the truckload. We got used to it. We even got a bit sick of it. They resented us for sheltering from the action, and we resented them for their unchanged dressings, their lopped-off legs, badly relidded heads, twisted mouths, missing noses: everything we didn't want to see and which they thrust in our faces. Soon there would be insults and sometimes fistfights.

In a way we were two towns then, two towns in the same place that turned their backs on each other, each with its promenades, its cafés, its hours. Two worlds. Only the widow Blachart reconciled them, opening her thighs to one and all, civilian and military, without rationing or discrimination, at every hour of the day or night. The line to her house sometimes reached ten metres; it was neutral territory, where men at odds could speak again, look at one another, fraternise while awaiting the great forgetfulness that holed up in the widow's belly. As for her, she spent the whole day — or just about — stretched out on the big bed, beneath her deceased husband's portrait. He was dressed for his wedding day, but black crêpe obscured his smile. It was only right, since every ten minutes an impatient guy took the place he'd deserted three years before, when a ton of coal fell on his head at the factory.

Old biddies used to curse the widow and spit at her back in the street. Agathe — that was her first name — didn't give a damn. After the war, some of those who received medals had not served as well as the widow had. We have to be fair. How many are even capable of offering their body and their warmth for a few coins?

In 1923, Agathe Blachart closed her shutters and her door, picked up a fairly light suitcase, and, saying goodbye to no one, left for V on the mail-coach. There she boarded the express for Chalons. At Chalons she changed trains, taking the one to Paris. Three days after that she was in Le Havre, where she set sail on the *Boréal*. Two months later she disembarked in Australia.

The books say that in Australia there are deserts, kangaroos, wild dogs, flat and limitless expanses, human beings who still live like cavemen, and cities new as coins from the mint. I'm not too sure we should believe them. Sometimes books lie. All I know for a fact is that the widow Blachart has been in Australia since 1923. Maybe she remarried over there. Maybe she even has children, a shop. Maybe everybody greets her with a respectful hello and a big smile. Maybe the oceans she put between herself and us enabled her to forget us completely — to be without past or sorrow, without anything.

Anyway, on the evening in question not all the wounded were at her place. The streets were full of them — flooded, actually — and most of them were tanked, hassling passers-by, yelling and vomiting, ganging up for trouble. To avoid them, Joséphine pulls her cart through the side streets. Instead of going down the rue du Pressoir, continuing on rue des Messiaux, skirting the church, coming back up behind city hall, and making a beeline to her shack towards the cemetery, she prefers to walk along the little canal, even though it's pretty narrow there — and she knows that with a full cart she'll have a hard time — even though this detour adds more than a kilometre.

It's cold. The frost makes everything crackle. Joséphine's nose is running and her flask is empty. The sky has become a roof of grey-blue tones that the first star pierces like a silver nail. The cart crushes the snow crust; the skins are stiff enough to stand like brooms. Joséphine raises a hand to wipe her nose, before an icicle can form. It's then and there that she sees in the distance, without any possible doubt, about sixty metres away — she swears it — young Morning Glory standing on the bank of the little canal, talking to a tall man bending down slightly to meet her. And this unmistakable figure in black, stiff as a living thing could be, standing by the little canal as the worn-out winter day prepares to take its leave, is none other than the prosecutor, Pierre-Ange Destinat himself. A testimony beyond the shadow of a doubt. Him, with the little girl, at the fall of night.

The two of them, him and her. Alone.

This twilight scene stopped Joséphine in her tracks. Why? No reason in particular. If we always had to explain everything we do, the gestures, the thoughts, the feelings, the movements, we'd never get to the end of it all. So Joséphine freezes in place like a pointer — what's odd about that? — on this Sunday, 2 December, as night falls, and that because she's just seen, straight ahead in the cold, the prosecutor of V chatting with a young flower, laying his hand on her shoulder — yes, his hand on her shoulder; she swears to that as well. 'Sixty metres away in the dark, a hand on a shoulder, when you're blind drunk? Come, now!' they'll tell her when they start harassing her later on — I'll come back to that. Joséphine doesn't give an inch. It was him. It was her. And no five sips of brandy could make her start seeing things!

So what? What's wrong with a conversation between Destinat and the little flower? He knew her. She knew him. To have seen them in this place where the next day she would be found strangled: what does that prove? Have we taken leave of our senses?

There was no more sound coming from the bedroom. Maybe Clémence had gone in and fallen asleep. Joséphine had finished her story and was looking at me. I was still seeing the

132

scene she'd just described, but Morning Glory had left the room, in silence, her drenched clothes clinging to her slim body of ice. She had smiled at me and disappeared.

★ ★ ★

'And then?' I ask Joséphine.

'Then what?'

'You went towards them?'

'Approach the prosecutor? I'm not crazy. I keep my distance from him.'

'And so?'

'So I turned back.'

'You left them like that?'

'What should I have done, set up a lantern for them and a foot warmer, perhaps?'

'And the little girl. You're sure it was her?'

'That golden-yellow hood of hers, how many of those do you see around? Anyway, I'd seen her sometimes going into her aunt's house. It was her for sure, you can take it from me.'

'What would she be doing at the edge of the canal?'

'Same as me, I'd guess: avoiding the drunks. A little ways further on, she would have come out on the square and taken the six o'clock mail-coach. You got anything to drink? All this talk is making me dry.'

★ ★ ★

I set out two glasses, a bottle, some cheese, a sausage and an onion. We drank and ate in silence. I looked at Joséphine as though to see through her the picture she'd painted for me. She nibbled like a mouse and drank big gulps of wine, making a fluent, pretty music with her tongue. Outside it was snowing heavily, not straight down but on a bias, against the window-panes, on which it seemed to be writing letters, letters that melted and streamed in rapid lines, like tears on an absent cheek. The weather was turning to muck. The frost was picking up its tattered finery and everything was dispersing. The next day would be all drips and mud.

It was late. In a corner of the kitchen, I laid out some blankets and a mattress. I'd succeeded in persuading Joséphine to go with me to V and tell everything to Mierck. We would leave at dawn. She nodded off almost immediately but slept fitfully, muttering things I couldn't make out. The big gun fired from time to time but without conviction — only to remind us it was there, like a bell of evil.

I didn't dare go back to the bedroom for fear of waking Clémence. I sat down in the armchair, the one I've still got, which holds

134

me like a big gentle hand. I closed my eyes.

We left at dawn. Clémence had got up and made us a full pot of coffee, boiling hot, and some mulled wine swirled into a bottle. At the door she gave us a little wave; but at me and me alone, she smiled. I took several steps towards her. I wanted so much to kiss her but felt embarrassed in front of Joséphine. So I returned her wave. And that's all.

Since then I haven't had a day without regret over that kiss I withheld.

'Have a nice trip,' she told me. Her last words, and my little gems. I still have them in my ear, intact; I play them every evening. *Have a nice trip.* I no longer have her face, but I swear I have her voice.

15

It took four hours to reach V. The horse kept bogging down in the mire, and the ruts were actually pits. In places the snow was melting like barrels that had been overturned, flooding the track until running water flowed into the ditches ahead and vanished. There were also convoys of troops heading to the front line — on foot, in carts, in trucks — obliging us to press up against the side to let them pass as best we could. We caught their melancholy gaze. Not a one of them reacted; not a one spoke, these denizens of the other world. Pale calves dressed in blue, meekly headed for the great abattoir.

Crusty, Judge Mierck's clerk, left us seated in an antechamber lined with red silk. I knew the room well. I had had frequent occasion to brood there about the universe — about boredom, the endlessness of an hour, a minute, a second. Without looking I could have drawn a perfect map of that room, showing the exact position of each piece of furniture, every decorative object, the number of petals on each dried anemone that sighed in the stoneware vase permanently set on the mantelpiece. Joséphine drowsed with her hands on her lap, waking abruptly from time to time as though struck by an electric shock.

After an hour Crusty reappeared, picking at his cheek. He'd evidently been at it since seating us, as there were lapels of dead skin on his black suit, which was worn to a shine at the elbows and knees. He showed us into the judge's office.

At first we almost couldn't see anything, but we heard two laughs. One, as thick as spit, I already knew. The other was totally unfamiliar, but I would get to know it soon enough. A haze of stinking smoke floated in the room, obscuring both the fat judge seated at his desk and the fellow standing near him. As my eyes grew accustomed to the pea soup, the judge's companion revealed himself. It was Matziev. They continued laughing, just as though we weren't there three steps in front of them. The officer was puffing on his cigar. The judge had his hands folded contentedly on his stomach. They were slow to let the laughter die, picking at the scraps of their joke. And when they were sure there was absolutely nothing left to laugh about, Mierck peered at us with his big, green, fish eyes.

'Well? What now?' The judge harrumphed in irritation, as if we had killed the gag. He was sizing up Joséphine as though I had come in with a head of livestock.

Mierck had no use for me, and the feeling was mutual. Our jobs — or, rather, my job and his *office* — often forced us into contact, but we never exchanged an unnecessary word. Our conversations were brief and without warmth, and when we spoke we hardly looked at each other.

I made the introductions, but before I could even summarise what Joséphine had told me, Mierck cut me short to address her.

'Profession?' Joséphine opened her mouth wide and thought for two or three seconds, but that was already too long for the judge. 'Is she an idiot or is she deaf? Profession?'

Joséphine cleared her throat, glanced at me, and at last spoke. 'Salvage dealer.'

The judge looked at the officer; they traded smiles. Finally, something else to laugh about. Then Mierck continued. 'And what is it she salvages?'

This was the judge's way of reducing people to nothing. He spoke as if you weren't there, as if you didn't exist, were something to be commented upon rather than addressed. He deleted people this way — with nothing but a pronoun. I've already said he knew how to use the language.

I saw Joséphine's face turn deep red, and her eyes held a glint of menace. I'm sure if she'd had her skinning knife to hand, she would have gutted Mierck right there without a second thought. She's not so strange that way. We kill a lot in the course of a day, in thought and in words, without fully realising it. In light of all these abstract crimes, actual murders are pretty rare when you consider it. In fact, it's only in wars that our actions keep up with our impulses.

Joséphine breathed deep and took the plunge. She stated her humble trade openly and clearly, without shame. Mierck resumed his petty abuse: 'Imagine that! In other words, she lives off carcasses!' He tried to coax a false laugh, intrusive as a tumour; it would have died if Matziev — still sucking on his cigar, as if only that kept the world spinning — had not ratified it and joined in.

I laid my hand on Joséphine's and started talking. Simply, without omitting any of the details, I recounted what she'd told me the night before. Mierck became serious again and listened without interrupting. When I had finished he looked up at the officer. They exchanged an inscrutable look. Then the judge picked up his letter opener with two fingers and set it dancing on its point on his desk blotter: a lively and nimble dance, between a polka and a quadrille, which ended as suddenly as it started. And that's when

Joséphine's torture truly began.

The judge and the colonel launched a joint offensive, without even conferring in advance. Men cut from the same cloth don't need to talk things over much in order to agree. Joséphine endured their broadsides painfully, sticking to her version; sometimes she looked over at me, with her eyes seeming to say, Why the hell did I listen to you? When are these bastards going to stop?

I couldn't do anything for her. I was just witnessing the sabotage. When Joséphine allowed in all innocence that she'd warmed herself several times with a sip from her brandy flask, Mierck and Matziev set about finishing her off. When they got through flaying her, she lowered her head, let out a long sigh, and looked at her hands, swollen from cold and work. In ten minutes she had aged twenty years.

Then they simply let up. You might have thought a game of cards had ended. Matziev lit another cigar and paced a few steps. Mierck leaned back in his chair and re-laced his fingers across the vest that covered his ballooning belly. It seemed my chance to speak now, but when I made to start, the judged stirred in his chair. 'Thank you. You're no longer needed. Dismissed! As for her, she'll remain until we can verify her statement.'

Joséphine turned to me, more frightened

than ever. Mierck got up to show me to the door. I laid a powerless hand on Joséphine's shoulder. In the antechamber, Crusty was dozing. Mierck signalled him to clear out, closed the doors again, and came up to me as he'd never done before, almost nose to nose, toe to toe. He spoke with a faint voice; I could see all the ruptured veins on his face and smell his breath: onions, fine wines soured, cured meats, and bitter coffee.

'You've been here a long time, so I'll excuse your zealousness in bringing that madwoman to my office to spout her drunken hallucinations. You meant no harm, I'm sure, but I've already informed you that Colonel Matziev is in charge of the inquiry. You'll take your orders from him. But if you breathe a word of this lunacy to the prosecutor, it won't go so easily for you next time. Now you can go.'

'And Madame Maulpas?' I said defiantly.

'Three days drying out in a cell should clear her head.'

He turned on his heel and went back in his office, leaving me standing there like a damn fool.

∗   ∗   ∗

'Three days?' Joséphine squawked. 'He held me for a week, that pig, on stale bread and pea soup brought to me by a battle-axe in a nun's habit . . . You sure he's dead?'

'Positive.'

'Better than he deserves! And the other one, the little shit with the cigar — is he dead?'

'I have no idea.'

★   ★   ★

We went on a lot longer, Joséphine and I, threading our way through the tangles of our lives. Talking of the distant past, we basked in the illusion that the game wasn't over yet, that there might yet be a place for us in the great mosaic of chance. And then, imperceptibly, we gravitated towards our childhood, towards the fragrant meadows where we played blind man's buff, the fears we shared, the songs, the water of the village springs. The steeple bell rang noon, but we could no longer tell whether it was the noon of our youth or that of the present, rasping and rusted over.

When Joséphine left, she kissed me on both cheeks. She'd never done that. I was grateful for that kiss. It sealed our kinship in a family of solitude, the cousinhood of a story that was old but still raw. She turned the corner of the street. And when I was alone, once again, my thoughts went back to Morning Glory.

Every Sunday the little girl had come to our town, ever since she was eight years old. Eight years then wasn't like eight years now. At eight you could handle almost anything, you had good sense and strong arms. You were almost an adult.

Bourrache had a flair for money. I've already said so. He'd chosen godparents for his daughters by following the scent of cash. That's why at her christening the little girl had found herself carried by a vague relation, an inhabitant of our town who by the time of the Case was pushing eighty. Adélaïde Siffert was her name. A tall woman once, she was all gnarled up, her face carved with a knife, her hands like a butcher's, her legs like a logger's: an old maid and glad of it but very good-hearted.

For forty years she'd been the bookkeeper at the town hall, less on account of any numerical skill than because she could handle pen and ink gracefully, without mistakes or smudges. On a small pension she managed to live if not indulgently then well enough, eating meat often and having her glass of port each evening.

So every Sunday, Bourrache sent the little girl to visit her godmother. She would arrive on the noon mail-coach and return on the six o'clock one. Adélaïde Siffert would serve a pork roast, green beans — fresh in season, from jars the rest of the year — a salad, and an apple cake. An unchanging menu; she told me herself. The little girl always had three helpings of cake. She told me that too. Then they would spend the afternoon sewing. Sometimes Morning Glory also did a bit of housecleaning. At five o'clock she would have another helping of cake, drink a cup of *café au lait*, and kiss her godmother, who would give her a five-franc note. The old woman would see her off. She had enjoyed her company, the little girl enjoyed her cake, and Bourrache would relish the five francs, which he would take from Morning Glory as soon as she returned. Everybody was content.

When the weather was bad, the little girl would stay the night at her godmother's house. There was never cause for concern: The next morning she would take the mail-coach, specifically the eight o'clock.

The evening of the crime — for according to Victor Desharet, who stuck his dirty paws into the child's body, opening her belly as you would unbutton a shirt, it was that very evening the crime was committed — Adélaïde had tried to keep the little girl with her. It was already cold enough to split a rock; you felt, drawing breath, like you were cracking apart from the inside. But the kid wouldn't be made to listen. 'I'm not cold, Godmother. Your hood keeps me warm as toast!' That had flattered the old lady, since she herself had made the hood, from velvet plush of a striking golden yellow, lined with rabbit fur. She'd given it to her for her seventh birthday. Morning Glory had drawn the strings and pulled on her mittens, and then, like a gust of wind, she'd hopped into the cold air and vanished.

Sorrow kills. In no time. The feeling of guilt does just as well, at least among those who have a shred of decency. Adélaïde Siffert followed her goddaughter to the cemetery. Twenty-two days between the two burials, not an hour more. And for those three weeks the tears flowed without end down Adélaïde's face, stopping neither by day, which I could witness, nor by night, as I'd be ready to swear. Good people go quickly. Everybody appreciates them — death, no less. Bastards, on the other hand, die old as a rule, and sometimes even in their beds, peaceful as can be.

Having left Joséphine in Judge Mierck's office, I didn't feel very proud of myself. I hung around V a while, hands in my pockets, my trousers getting filthier by the minute from all the mud splattering the pavements.

The city was giddy, a city of drunks. Recruits stamped here and there, glutting the streets with their asinine jokes and horsing around. A new batch, sizable this time, were gearing up to have a go at the Krauts, and for now they could all still laugh about it. The streets as well as the cafés were given over to uniforms: a river of brand-new leggings, shiny buttons, smartly sewn epaulettes. Here they were singing, there they were yelling — or whistling at the few girls who hurried past into the stores. It was like the onset of a rutting season — massive, wild, communal and bloody — a thrust of raw life you could feel welling up, on the verge of gushing out.

I wondered what I could come up with to do among all these suckers who hadn't figured out the score. Soon enough, most of them would be making the trip back packed in four lousy planks of larch, if they were lucky enough for someone to find their scraps at the bottom of a shell crater or dangling from barbed wire.

Drifting along, walking like a blind man, I ended up at the door of the Rébillon. I was taken aback. Then I thought that this was the only place I could have gone: I had to come here and push the door open to see Bourrache, with his dark eyes and hulking frame, had to shake his hand and mumble the stupid words you say on such occasions.

Never before had I seen the big dining room empty. Not a sound. Not a single table set. Not a voice. No tinkle of glass or silver. No pipe smoke. No smell of food. Just a meagre fire in the enormous hearth, and Bourrache before it, seated on a foot-stool, his feet stretched towards the few live embers, his head hunched over: a lifeless giant.

He hadn't heard me come in. I stood near him and spoke the practised words. He didn't move, made no reply. I watched the fire fall back; the last beautiful flames shrank and twisted, still struggling to stay erect, until they finally suffocated and disappeared. Then I saw the gaze of Clémence, her eyes and her smile. I saw her belly. I saw my shameless happiness and I saw the face of Morning Glory, not dead and drenched but as I'd glimpsed her for the last time in this very dining room, alive and rosy and lush as young wheat, slipping between the tables to bring the patrons their pitchers of Toul and Vic.

The flames had given way to acrid grey fumes that escaped from the hearth, jigged around the room, and crashed into the darkened ceiling. At that point Bourrache, slow as an exhausted ox, turned his face towards me — a face that showed no feeling or expression. Then he got up, reached for my neck with his massive hands, and started to squeeze and squeeze, harder and harder — but strangely, I wasn't afraid. I let him do it: I knew I wasn't dealing with a murderer, nor even with a madman, but simply a father who'd just lost his child and for whom the world was now like a huge sun spotted with black. I felt myself choking. Everything was buzzing inside me. I saw before me white dots, flashes, and the scarlet features of Bourrache, who trembled, trembled — and suddenly tore his hands from my neck as though from a red-hot iron, fell to the floor, and cried.

I caught my breath again. I was dripping with sweat. I lifted Bourrache and helped him to the nearest table. He offered no resistance. He was sobbing and sniffling. I knew where the bottles of plum brandy were kept. I went and fetched one, along with two glasses I filled to the brim. I helped him drink his, then knocked mine back, followed by another. Like a robot, Bourrache poured himself three, tossing them down in single gulps. I saw his eyes gradually refocus on our world and look at me with surprise, as if wondering what on earth I was doing there. A prick soldier tapped on the windowpane right beside us. Clownishly, he peered into the room, pressing his nose against the glass. But then he saw us. He lost his grin and was gone. I stayed there for four hours. Four hours and two bottles of booze. Four hours and hardly three words. I thought it was the very least I could do.

During that time, Clémence was beginning to groan and writhe, alone. Without me. Without my knowing it.

16

When I came out of the Rébillon, a frigid rain braced me somewhat. The sky seemed to have it in for all mankind. Massive bands of water lashed the façades. There weren't too many people in the streets. I hugged the walls as best I could, using my hands to shield my eyes at least. Joséphine in her cell was no doubt cursing me now, I thought, calling me every name in her substantial arsenal of insults. I believe I even smiled a little over that.

By the time I reached the post office, I was drenched. My feet were numb, but at least my mind was clear again. My head wasn't spinning any longer, despite the brandy. The mail-coach was there, and a great many people were gesticulating around it; a captain of the corps of engineers was trying to make himself heard. I drew closer. The officer's attempt to reason with the crowd provoked some menacing stances among the men. The women, more reasonable or simply resigned, stood around waiting like cattle, indifferent to the downpour. At that point somebody laid a hand on my shoulder. It was our parish priest, Father Lurant. 'There's no way back for us. The road's been commandeered for the convoys. Two regiments are headed for the front tonight.'

I hadn't noticed them initially. But as soon as the priest pointed them out I could see nothing but the dozens — hundreds — of men, maybe more, waiting in utter silence, rifles on their shoulders and kits on their backs. They seemed to encircle us, almost blending into the night, which had begun to lap at day. Standing there with absent eyes, without a gesture, without a word, like the womenfolk, they were indifferent to the rain. You might have taken them for an army of shadows. And yet they were the same lads who'd roamed around V all day long, heading towards the cafés like animals to a water trough, belting out songs, spewing obscenities, unbuttoning themselves in the bordellos, staggering with wine bottles in hand. Now, not a one of them was laughing. All were leaden as toy soldiers, in both their bearing and their colour.

'Come,' the priest said. 'There's no point in standing around.' I followed him as submissively as any recruit.

It wasn't the first time that staff headquarters had commandeered the road. I have to say it was very narrow and in a sorry state, after three years of passing trucks and the hooves of thousands of nags. So when they were gearing up for an offensive there was really no choice but to reserve it for the convoys, which proceeded sometimes all day and all night, without interruption, a sad jolting line of ants, filing slowly towards the gutted remains of their anthill of metal and earth.

Father Lurant took me along to the bishop's palace, where a caretaker let us in. The priest explained the situation, and without comment the man led us, through a labyrinth of hallways and staircases redolent of wax and soft soap, to a large room where two rickety iron beds were making conversation.

When I saw the small beds I thought of ours, so big and so deep. I'd rather have been beside Clémence, seeking that sweetness in her arms I always knew how to find there. I asked if I might send her word, which I did as a rule whenever I couldn't get home. In such cases I would call the mayor, who would send his maid Louisette with the message. But the caretaker recommended I save myself the trouble: The telephone lines, like the road, were commandeered until further notice. A pang went through me to imagine Clémence worrying, but there was nothing to be done about it. With luck I'd be back in time for lunch tomorrow.

The priest undressed, with no ado. He removed his cape, then his cassock, and stood before me in his underwear, his belly sticking out before him like a gigantic quince swinging in a flannel hammock. He arranged his damp clothes near the oven and huddled near it, spreading his hands at intervals over the lid. Without his clothes, he seemed not as old as I had thought. No doubt he was my own age, but I had never seen him as a man before. He must have suspected everything I was thinking. Priests are very clever; they know exactly how to enter people's heads. He looked at me, smiling as the heat made his cape smoke like a censer, and his drying cassock filled the air with the scents of humus and burnt wool.

The caretaker returned with two bowls of soup, a big loaf of brown bread, a piece of cheese hard as a block of oak, and a jug of wine. He left all of it on a little table and bade us goodnight. I undressed and laid my outer clothes near the fire as well. They produced scorched odours of wood and suint that mixed with those of the priest's clothing.

We ate earnestly, with no care for our manners. Father Lurant's hands were large, hairless, and plump. Whatever he put in his mouth he chewed for an age, and he drank the wine with his eyes shut. We finished everything. We left the table clean, our stomachs full. Then, dressed as equals, we set about talking as we'd never done before. We talked about flowers — they were his passion — 'the most glorious proof, if one needed any, of God's existence,' he said. It seemed odd even then: talking about flowers in that room while the night and the war surrounded us, while somewhere nearby the villain who'd strangled a ten-year-old girl roamed free or slept in his bed. It seems ludicrous now as I imagine Clémence lying in our bed at that moment, bleeding helplessly.

I didn't know you could talk so about flowers. I mean, I didn't know you could talk about human beings while speaking of nothing but flowers, without mentioning the words *man*, *destiny*, *death* and *loss*. I found out that evening. The priest knew the science of words — like Mierck, like Destinat — but unlike those two, he did beautiful things with them. He rolled them like cigarettes with his tongue, and all at once a nothing appeared to be a marvel. They must teach such things in the seminaries: how to catch the imagination with a few well-turned phrases. He told me about his garden, which we never saw because of the high walls that enclosed it behind the presbytery. He told me about the chamomiles, the hellebores, the petunias, the sweet williams, the wild pinks, the anemones, the sedums, the candy-tufts, the peonies, the Syrian opals, the daturas, the flowers that live for only a season, the ones that come back year after year, the ones that open only in the evening and vanish in the morning, and the ones that beam from dawn to dusk, displaying their delicate corollas of rosy or mauve convolvulus, only to close abruptly at nightfall, as if a wrathful hand had squeezed their velvet petals and choked them.

The priest spoke of these last in a different tone from the others. Not as a priest any more — not as a horticulturalist either — but as a man full of misery and wounds. I cut him off as he was about to name this flower aloud, in the darkened room. I didn't want to hear that name. For two days it had been drumming in my head. The little girl's face came back to me like a slap across the face. The priest fell silent, perhaps a bit embarrassed. Outside, the rain had turned to snow again, and the flakes crowded against the windowpane like fireflies of ice. Without life and without light, for two or three seconds they yet managed to give the illusion of life and light.

Afterwards, for years, I tried to get morning

glories to grow in our little garden. I never succeeded. The seeds stayed in the ground, and there they stubbornly rotted, refusing to climb towards the sky, to issue from the humid, gluey dark mass. Only the couch grass and thistles flourished, invading everything, growing incredibly high, spreading over the few square yards with their dangerous corollas. In the end I let them have their way.

I've often thought back to the priest's comment about flowers, God, and proof. And I've said to myself that there are undoubtedly places in the world where God never sets foot.

Father Lurant went off to evangelise the tribes of Annam, in the mountains of Indochina. That was in 1925. He stopped by to let me know. I really don't know why he troubled himself. Maybe it was because one day the two of us had talked for a long time in our underpants, had shared the same room and the same wine. I didn't question his decision to go — just like that — even though he was hardly a young man by then. I simply asked, 'And your flowers?'

He looked at me, smiling, now as ever since our talk with that priestly gaze designed to reach in and pull out our souls like a cooked snail from its shell. He told me that where he was going there were thousands of flowers, thousands he didn't know, that he'd never seen, except in books, and you couldn't live forever in books: One day you had to take a firm hold of life and its beauties.

I was about to tell him I took the opposite view: I had had it up to here with life, and if there were books where I could live I would plunge right into them. But when two people are so far apart, there's no point debating it. I held my tongue and wished him well on his trip.

After that, I can't say that I thought of him often. But sometimes I did. Edmond Gachentard, my old colleague, had given me a few images of those eastern lands, in addition to his rifle. I'm not talking about images on paper, I mean the ones that get inside your head and stay there.

In his youth, Gachentard had belonged to the expeditionary corps sent to Tonkin. Apart from the fever that would suddenly turn him white as a leek, he returned with a jar of green coffee he would keep on his dining room table like a relic, a photograph of himself in uniform with rice paddies in the background, and above all a slowness in his eyes, a kind of absence that seized him whenever he spoke about them: the nighttime melodies of bullfrogs; the incessant stickiness of the body; the great muddy river carrying trees as well as goat carcasses, water lilies and bindweed torn from its banks. At times Gachentard even mimicked the women's dances for me, their graceful hand movements with curved fingers, the rolling of their eyes, and the flute music too, which he re-created by whistling as he pretended to play on the sawed-off handle of a broom.

I sometimes visualised the priest in that setting: his arms full of unknown flowers, wearing a colonial hat and a tropical cassock — hemmed at the bottom by a scallop of dry mud — watching the warm rain fall on glossy forests. I would see him smiling. Always smiling. I don't know why.

★   ★   ★

When I awoke in the room at the bishop's palace, I had an insistent thought of Clémence. I had to get home, at all costs — leave right away, bypass the road if it was still off limits — nothing mattered but to get back to her. I can't say it was a premonition. I wasn't worried. No, I simply had the most urgent need for her skin and her eyes, I wanted to hold her and briefly forget the works of death everywhere around me.

I put on my clothes, not quite dry. I filled the basin and scrubbed my face. Father

Lurant was still dead to the world, a broad smile on his face. Beaming, really. I figured that even in his sleep, he must be finding armfuls of flowers. Looking at the table, I remembered we had finished every scrap from the night before, so I took off on an empty stomach.

★   ★   ★

Berthe is in the kitchen. I can't see her, but I sense her huffing and shaking her head in disgust. Whenever she sees my notebooks, she huffs. What's it to her how I spend my days? It must be the mere markings that bother her. She's never learned to read. For her these lined-up words are a great mystery. Fear and envy, perhaps.

But whose, really? Now I am coming to the point I've been eyeing for months, for the longest while visible but not yet present. Like a dreadful horizon, a disfigured hill: Behind its hideous face, you don't know what might be hiding.

I am coming to that miserable morning. To that point when all pendulums stop. To that infinite fall. To the death of the stars.

When all is said and done, Berthe isn't wrong. Words are frightening, even to those who know and can decipher them. Here I am, a man in his fifties, flailing like a teenager trying to express himself. I don't know how to do it on the best of days. Today it's hard just holding the pen. As soon as I pick it up, my insides get knotted, my eyes sting. I drink a glass of wine. Then another, knocking it back. Maybe what's said about writers is true: words come out of the bottle. I grab my bottle and gulp it all down. I can feel Clémence draw near, her breath, always young, stirring the grey hairs on the back of my neck.

'Drinking so much in the morning — you should be ashamed. You'll be drunk before noon!'

Berthe. I tell her off. *Mind your own business.* She answers with an indifferent shrug and leaves me. I take a deep breath. I pick up my pen again.

★ ★ ★

My heart swelled unbearably when I saw the house, the roof's edge fringed with tapers of ice. It was completely covered with snow, glistening under a bright sun swaggering low in the sky. Suddenly I wasn't cold or hungry any longer; I'd forgotten the forced march that took four hours along the shoulder of the road, on which the conga line of soldiers, carts, cars, and trucks never let up. I must have passed hundreds of guys trudging solemnly along, glaring at me in my civvies and at my impatience to move in the direction they dreaded going.

I knocked my clodhoppers on the wall, less to get rid of the snow than to make some noise, a familiar noise that would say I was there, on the other side of the wall, a couple of steps, a few seconds away. I smiled as I imagined Clémence imagining me. I took hold of the latch, pushed the door open. There was no war at that moment. There was no ghost, no murdered child. There was only the prospect of Clémence and of our baby to be felt under her skin.

Life is strange. It doesn't give you warnings. It jumbles everything so you can't pick and choose, and bloody moments follow moments of grace, just like that. It can make you wonder if man isn't like one of those pebbles that lie on the road, lying in the same place for entire days until someone kicks it and sends it sailing through the air for no reason. And what can a pebble do?

In the house there was a strange silence that slackened my smile: an impression that it had been uninhabited for weeks. Things were in their place but seemed heavier and colder. Above all, this great silence permeated the walls and drowned my voice when I called out. And then: at the top of the staircase, the door to the bedroom was ajar, as it never would have been; and I felt my heart go wild. I took a couple of steps until an irrational dread kept me from going any further.

I no longer recall the sequence of what came next or the time of my movements. Clémence was on the bed, her forehead colourless and her lips paler still. The colour had left her with the blood that was everywhere. From the grip of her hands on her belly, it seemed as if she had been trying all on her own to bring into the world what she'd carried for months. Around her reigned the greatest disorder, evidence of her efforts, her falls. She hadn't managed to open the window to call for help. She hadn't even tried to go downstairs — for fear, no doubt, of pitching over and losing the child. And so she ended up stretched out on the bed, breathing with a dreadful slowness, the warmth almost gone from her cheeks. I pressed my lips to hers and said her name; I shouted it, I held her face in my hands, I slapped it, I breathed air into her mouth. The child that had filled my thoughts all these months was gone from my mind; I must admit that. I thought only of her. I tried the window. The handle came off in my hand, and when I broke the pane with my fist, I let my blood mingle with hers, until

I found myself imagining us both bled dry, our life soaked up by the bedclothes. I howled at the street, howled with all the anger of a mistreated animal. Doors opened, windows. I fell to the floor, but even on my knees I still had the sensation of falling. For me there has been no more living except in that fall.

17

Hippolyte Lucy stands near Clémence, bending over her, with his anxious face and all his instruments. They've sat me down on a chair. I look on without comprehending. There are a lot of people in the room: neighbouring women, old and young, speaking in low tones as if it's already a wake. Where were all these bitches when Clémence was in agony, calling for help? Tell me. Where were these females who've shown up now, feeding on misfortune under my nose? I get up abruptly, like a murderer, a lunatic. I see them recoil. I kick them out. I close the door. Now there's just the three of us: Clémence, the doctor, and me.

As I've said, Hippolyte Lucy was a good doctor. A good doctor and a decent man. I couldn't see what he was doing, but I knew he was doing all he could. He said words to me: *haemorrhage, coma.* He told me to hurry. I lifted Clémence. She weighed nothing. It seemed that only her belly was still alive, that life had taken refuge in that swollen belly, ravenous, starving.

I held her close to me in the carriage while

the doctor cracked his whip at the rump of his two nags. We arrived at the clinic. There they separated me from her. Two nurses wheeled her away on a trolley. Clémence glided off into odours of ether, crinkles of white sheets.

For hours I stayed there, waiting beside a soldier who'd lost his left arm. I remember his obscene contentment to have lost only an arm, especially the left one — a real piece of luck since he was right-handed. In six days he'd be home for good. Far from this war for dupes, as he said. One arm lost, many years won. Years of life. He never stopped reminding himself as he gestured with his stump. He'd even given a name to that absent limb — Gugusse — from time to time addressing it, calling it to bear witness: 'Farewell, Gugusse. Isn't that right, Gugusse?' Happiness doesn't depend on much. Sometimes it hangs by a thread, sometimes by an arm. War is the world turned on its head; it can make an amputee the happiest of men.

His name was Léon Castrie, that happy soldier. He was from the Morvan. He caused me to smoke a lot of cigarettes. He got me drunk on words, and I really needed that. He never asked me a question. He didn't need me to make conversation. He made it all alone with his phantom limb. When they called his name, he stood up and said, 'We have to go. Come along, Gugusse!' It was suppertime. Léon Castrie, thirty-one years old, corporal in the 127th, from the Morvan, bachelor, farmer. He loved life and cabbage soup. That's what I remember.

A nurse came. It was evening by then. She said the child had been saved; I could go see him if I wanted to. I shook my head. I said it was Clémence I wanted to see. I asked for news. The nurse said I still had to wait, she would go and ask the doctor. Off she went again.

Later, the doctor came — a military doctor, exhausted, worn out, overwhelmed. He might have been a butcher, a steer slaughterer, to judge by his bloody apron, his cap as well. For days he'd been operating without let-up, creating Gugusses on an assembly line; some left happy, more of them dead, all of them black and blue. To him a young woman was an aberration in the midst of all that male carnage. He talked to me about the baby, so big he couldn't come out all by himself. Everything was fine with him. Then he gave me a cigarette. A bad sign: I knew those cigarettes all too well, having given out quite a few myself, to guys who didn't have many more days of life or of freedom. We smoked without speaking. And as he exhaled, evading my eyes, he murmured, 'She lost a lot of blood . . . ' His sentence hung in the air with the smoke. It didn't dissipate. And with that I understood the blood covering him to be Clémence's blood. This poor fellow with rings under his eyes and a three-day beard, who got tangled in his own sentences, this poor, tired, valiant man who had done everything humanly possible — I suddenly felt the urge to kill him. This shocked me. Even with violent means always available, I'd never had such a strong desire to kill somebody with my own two hands. To kill with rage, to kill with savagery.

'I have to go back,' he said, snuffing his cigarette on the floor. Then he innocently laid a hand on my murderous arm. 'You can go and see her,' he continued. And off he went, with a weary slowness.

★ ★ ★

The world doesn't stop turning just because some of us are suffering. And bastards will be bastards, no matter what. Maybe there's no such thing as chance. I've often told myself that. We're all centred on our own tragedies. Morning Glory, Destinat, Joséphine in her jail cell, Mierck and Matziev — all forgotten.

At the very time when I should have been there, I wasn't, and the two creeps made the most of my absence to do their dirty work unhindered, almost as if they'd ordered Clémence's death to get me out of the way and give them room to manoeuvre. That's what they did. With no shame.

As you can imagine, a crime such as the Case can really shake up a region. Such news ripples like a wave that makes everything tremble in its path. It fills people's heads with horror and their mouths with talk, both at once. You might say it sets their minds fretting and their tongues wagging. In all, it's no good for anyone to know that a murderer is roaming the countryside, that he could be right under your nose, that maybe your paths have crossed, or will, that maybe he's your neighbour. It's especially bad during a war, when all you have is what little peace and quiet can be found on the home front. If not, all is lost.

There aren't umpteen ways to solve a murder. I only know of two: Either you arrest the culprit or you arrest somebody you say is the culprit. One or the other. Not much more to it than that. Either way, it's the same so far as the population is concerned. The only loser on the deal is the guy who's arrested; but when all is said and done, who cares what he thinks? Now, if there are more crimes, that's a different story, true enough. But that wasn't the case in our town. Little Morning Glory remained the only girl who was strangled. There were no others. Proof positive for those who needed any that we'd got our man. Case closed. Pass the salt!

What I'm going to tell about now I didn't see with my own eyes, but that doesn't change anything. I've spent years tying the threads together, retrieving the words, the trails, the questions and answers. It's as near as I can get to the truth. I haven't made anything up. Why would I?

18

On that morning while I was crawling back home along the road from the bishop's palace, the police arrested two young lads, half dead from hunger and exposure. Two deserters from the 59th Infantry. They weren't the first the mounted police had caught in their net. For several months now, things had begun to unravel. Men fled the front line every day and vanished into the countryside, at times preferring to die all alone in the thickets and copses than be blown apart by the shells. Let's just say that these two could not have come along at a better time. It suited everybody: the army, which needed to make an example of someone, and the judge, who needed a culprit.

The two kids were paraded through the streets, between two swaggering policemen. People came out to see them: two fools and two officers. Two ragged bums, scraggly and unshaven, uniforms in tatters, eyes rolling every which way, stomachs empty, dragging their feet, towed by two big gendarmes, ruddy and well-fed, polished boots, pressed trousers, the picture of conquerors.

The crowd swelled for no apparent reason, maybe because a crowd is stupid by nature. It closed in on the prisoners with more and more menace. Fists were raised; insults flew, rocks too. What's a crowd? A gathering of people, every one of whom would prove to be a goose if you looked him in the eye and talked to him alone. But put together, almost stuck to one another, amid the odour of bodies, of sweat, of breath, a look, the merest word, right or wrong, turns into dynamite; a crowd becomes a hellish machine, a grenade without its pin.

The policemen saw how the wind was blowing. They picked up their pace. The deserters necessarily did likewise. All four took refuge in the town hall, where the mayor soon joined them. A calming wave was produced. A city hall is almost like a church — but a church with the blue, white, and red always hanging on the façade and the lovely motto nicely sculpted for first-rate fools: LIBERTY, EQUALITY, FRATERNITY. The stone façade of official order cooled the passions of the would-be rioters. Everybody stopped short, fell silent, and waited.

After a while the mayor came out, clearing his throat. You could see that fear was working on his guts. Despite the cold, he was mopping his forehead; then he spoke.

'Everything is under control. You can all go back home!' he said.

'We want them,' answered a voice.

'Who do you mean?' the mayor replied.

'The murderers!' called a voice, not the same as the first, backed up right away by a dozen more in succession, like an evil echo.

'What murderers?' asked the mayor.

'The murderers of the little girl!'

The mayor was aghast but pulled himself together. He told them they were nuts, this was all nonsense; these two fellows were deserters, the gendarmes would be turning them over to the army, and the army would know how to deal with them.

'It's them — we want them!' some numbskull repeated.

'Well, you're not getting them,' answered the mayor, stubborn and furious by now. 'I've notified the judge, and he's on his way!'

★   ★   ★

There are magic words. *Judge* is a magic word. Like *God, death, child*, and a number of others. They're words that command respect, whatever your other feelings. *Judge* can send a chill down your spine, even when you've done nothing wrong, particularly when it has a face and the face is like the one

172

these people knew. These people knew very well that the judge was Mierck. The incident of the 'little worlds' had festered in people's minds — what kind of person would stuff himself with soft-boiled eggs next to a corpse? — not to mention the contempt he showed for the little girl, not a word, no expression of pity. But it didn't matter that they hated him, he was still the judge: the man who, with an indifferent stroke of the pen, could send you off to think things over behind bars. The man who made small talk with the executioner. He loomed in their nightmares as the bogeyman loomed in their children's.

People looked at one another. The crowd started dispersing, slowly at first, then very quickly, as though seized by a sudden belly-ache. When only a dozen hotheads remained, standing on the cobblestones like so many iron pokers, the mayor turned his back on them and went back in.

His bright idea had undoubtedly prevented a lynching. But now the mayor really did have to notify the judge.

Mierck arrived in the early afternoon, accompanied by Matziev. It seems they were already getting on like long-lost friends, which didn't surprise me, since I'd seen them at it before, and afterwards too. I think I've already said they were cut from the same

173

dirty cloth. They made their way to the town hall, where they established an armed camp with the support of a dozen policemen who'd come for that very purpose. The judge's first order was to require that two good armchairs be placed before the fireplace in the mayor's office and that wine be brought as well as something to go with it, cheese and white bread. The mayor sent Louisette to look for the best she could find.

Matziev got out one of his cigars. Mierck looked at his watch and whistled. The mayor remained standing, not too sure of what to do. The judge gave him a nod, which he took as an order to fetch the two deserters and their guards. And that he did.

The poor fellows entered the room, and the good fire restored some of their colour. The colonel told the gendarmes to 'go outside and see if I'm there', which made Mierck laugh. And so the two inquisitors set about sizing up those two kids. I say kids, because take away a few years and that's what they were. One of them, Maurice Rifolon, aged twenty-two, born in Melun, resident of Paris, 15 rue des Amandiers, in the 20th arrondissement, had been a typographer. The other, Yann Le Floc, aged twenty, born in Plouzagen — a Breton village he'd never left before the war — was a farmhand.

'What struck me,' the mayor confessed

later, much later, 'was the difference between them. The little Breton kept his head down. You could clearly see he was consumed by fear. Whereas the other one, the city fellow, looked us straight in the eye, almost with a smile but not quite. It was like he didn't give a damn about us or about anything.'

★ ★ ★

The colonel opens fire first. 'You know why you're here?' he asks them.

Rifolon stares at him, doesn't answer. The little Breton lifts his head a bit and mumbles, 'Because we left, Colonel, sir. Because we ran away.'

Mierck joins the fray. 'Because you killed.'

The little Breton's eyes widen. On the other hand, cool as can be, Rifolon remarks, 'Of course we killed; that's why they came to get us, so we could kill more men across from us who look like our brothers, to kill them so they'll kill us. It's people like you who put us up to it — '

The little Breton panics. 'I'm not so sure I killed anybody. Maybe not, maybe I missed them; it's pretty hard to see, and I don't know how to shoot, even my corporal makes fun of me. 'Le Floc,' he says, 'you couldn't hit a cow in a hallway!' '

The colonel goes up to them. He takes a big drag on his cigar and exhales the smoke into their faces. The little one coughs. The other doesn't bat an eyelid. 'It's a little girl you killed, a ten-year-old girl.'

The little Breton jumps. 'What? What? What?' It seems he repeated the word at least twenty times, hopping in place, wriggling like a man on fire.

As for the typographer, he retained his calm and his slight mocking smile. He was the one the judge addressed now. 'You don't seem surprised?'

He took his time about answering; he examined Mierck from head to foot and Matziev too. The mayor told me, 'He looked like he was weighing them with his eyes, and he seemed amused by all this!'

Finally he answers. 'Nothing surprises me any longer. If you had seen what I've seen these past months, you'd know that anything is possible.' A pretty turn of phrase, no? And a smack in the face for the judge, who starts to turn crimson.

'You deny it?' he shouts.

'On the contrary, I confess,' the other quietly replies.

'What?' yells the small one, grabbing his pal's collar. 'Are you crazy? What are you talking about? Don't listen to this guy! I don't

176

know him; we've only been together since last night! Me, I don't know what he did. Bastard, why are you doing this? Tell them, go on, tell them!'

Mierck shuts him up by sequestering him in a corner of the office, as though to say, We'll see about you later. Then he comes back to the other one. 'You were saying?'

'Whatever you want,' he says, peaceful as ever.

'The little girl?'

'I killed her. I'm the one. I saw her. I followed her. I stabbed her in the back three times with a knife.'

'No, you strangled her.'

'Yes, that's right, I strangled her, with these very hands. You're right, I didn't have a knife.'

'On the bank of the little canal.'

'Exactly.'

'And you put her in the water.'

'Yes.'

'Why did you do that?'

'Felt like it.'

'You wanted to rape her?'

'Yes.'

'But she wasn't raped.'

'Didn't have time. There was some noise. I ran off.'

The lines flow without hesitation, as at the theatre — that's how the mayor put it. The typographer stands very straight, speaks very clearly. The judge doesn't miss a beat. You'd think they'd been rehearsing for hours. The little Breton cries, his face full of snot, heaving his shoulders and shaking his head continuously in futile dissent. Matziev envelops himself in the smoke of his cigar.

The judge addresses the mayor. 'You're a witness to these confessions?'

This takes the mayor aback. He knows full well he's witnessed no such thing. He knows Mierck realises this too. And to top it off, he knows the judge doesn't give a damn what he thinks. Mierck has what he wants, and the likes of the mayor won't be snatching it away from him.

'Can we really say confessions ... ' ventures the mayor.

Matziev gets into the act. 'You have ears, Mayor, and a brain. So you've heard them and understood them.'

'Perhaps you would like to lead the inquiry?' the judge says, backing up the colonel. And with that the mayor falls silent.

The little Breton is still crying. The other one stands straight as a flagpole, now smiling broadly, elsewhere already. Anyway, he'd figured it out. Deserter: shot. Murderer: executed. Either way, so long! All he wanted was to go quickly. That's all. And why not

178

make things difficult for everyone in the process?

Mierck called back one of the policemen, who conducted the typographer upstairs to a narrow room, a broom closet. He was locked inside and the gendarme stood guard at the door.

The judge and the colonel decided to reward their own efficiency with a break, so they gave the mayor to understand they'd call him when they needed him. The tearful little Breton was led down to the cellar by another policeman, and since the cellar couldn't be locked, he was handcuffed and made to sit on the floor. The rest of the squad returned to the scene of the crime, on Mierck's orders, to go over it with a fine-tooth comb.

It was already fairly late in the afternoon. Louisette came back with a lot of provisions she'd collected here and there. The mayor told her to serve those gentlemen — and, not a mean man, he told her to take a little something to the prisoners as well.

'At the time my brother was at the front,' Louisette would tell me. 'I knew it was tough; he'd had the same idea as them. 'You'll hide me!' he'd told me one day when he'd come on leave, and I told him, No, if he did that I'd tell the mayor and the police.' She wouldn't have done it, but she knew what happened to deserters and wanted to frighten him. In the end he died anyway, a week before the armistice. 'All that to tell you I felt sorry for those poor guys, so before I served those two healthy men, I took food to the prisoners. The one in the cellar was huddling in terror. He wouldn't take the bread and bacon; I left everything beside him on a barrel. As to the other one in the closet upstairs, I knocked on the door. There wasn't any answer. I knocked again: still nothing. I had my arms full of the bread and bacon, so the policeman opened the door. The poor guy was smiling — I swear, he was smiling, staring us right in the face, his eyes open wide. I screamed and dropped everything. The policeman said 'Shit!' and pounced on him. But it was too late. He'd used his trousers to hang himself; he'd made strips of them and tied them to the handle of the transom window. I wouldn't have thought an old window handle was that strong.'

Mierck and Matziev took the news in their stride. 'Further proof, as if any were needed!' they said to the mayor. They looked at each other knowingly.

Night was beginning to fall. The colonel added logs to the fire, and the judge summoned Louisette. She arrived with her head lowered, trembling all over. She thought he was going to question her about the suicide. Mierck asked what she'd found for them to eat. She reported. 'Three sausages, some potted meat, some ham, some pigs' trotters, a chicken, some calves' liver, a cow's-milk cheese, and a goat cheese.' He was obviously content and gave his orders without a moment's thought: the pork products as an appetiser, braised calves' liver after that, then a stew of chicken, cabbage, carrots, onions, sausage, followed by pigs' trotters à l'estouffade, the cheeses, and an apple crêpe. And wine, of course, the best available. White with the first course, red after that. And with the back of his hand, he sent her off to her kitchen.

Throughout the evening, Louisette shuttled between the town hall and the mayor's house: bringing bottles and tureens, removing the empties, serving the next course, carrying off the dishes of the preceding one. The mayor had taken to his bed with a sudden fever. They had unhooked the typographer and taken him to the hospital morgue. A single gendarme had stayed behind at the town hall, to keep watch on the little Breton. Louis Despiaux was the gendarme's name, a fine fellow; I'll come back to him.

The mayor's office, where the judge and the colonel had bivouacked, looked out onto a small courtyard, where a skinny chestnut tree had grown very tall. From one of the office windows you could see it perfectly: a scrawny thing that never had room to flourish and become a real tree. It's been gone a long time now. Shortly after the Case, the mayor had it cut down, finding that when he looked at it he saw something besides a sick tree, something he couldn't stomach. From the office you reached the courtyard by a low door that closed a corner. On the door, spines of books were outlined in *trompe l'oeil*; this beautiful design augmented one's impression of the library, which was otherwise pretty threadbare and held precious few real books — never opened — alongside tomes of the civil and the municipal codes. At the end of the courtyard there were toilets and a canopy wide as a man's outstretched arms, under which logs were stacked.

When Louisette brought the ham and potted meat she was welcomed with a cry of contentment; then, though she couldn't recall it exactly, a pleasantry by the colonel in her regard that made the judge laugh. She placed the plates, the silverware, the glasses, and all the clink-clank on a round table and served. The colonel threw his cigar into the fire and sat down first, after asking her name. He supposedly remarked, 'Louisette: a very lovely name for a very lovely girl.' And Louisette supposedly smiled, pocketing the compliment — unaware the dandy was making fun of her, with her three missing teeth and her eyes slightly at odds with each other. Then the judge spoke. He asked her to go down to the cellar and advise the guard that they needed to talk with the prisoner. Louisette left the office, trembling as though she were going to Hades. The little Breton had stopped crying, but he hadn't touched the bread and bacon. Louisette delivered the message, but the prisoner was unresponsive, and Despiaux had to grab him by the handcuffs and frog-march him upstairs.

★   ★   ★

I tracked Despiaux down not long ago. He told me his story on the terrace of the Café de la Croix at V. The weather was mild. It was a June evening, June 21. After the notorious night I'm about to describe, he left the police force and headed south, where a brother-in-law of his had a vineyard. After that he went on to Algeria, where he worked for a maritime trading post that stocked ships with provisions. He came back to V early in 1921 and still serves as an assistant accountant at Carbonnieux, the department store. A good job, he says. He's a tall fellow, quite slender but not skinny, his face still very young, though his hair is as white as flour. As he remembered it, his hair went white all at once after the night with the little Breton. But who knows? In his gaze one sensed some kind of void. The closer one came to it, the further away it would float. Yet it beckoned to be explored, though you'd hesitate for fear of getting lost in it. He told me, 'The kid, who hadn't said two words, had cried his eyes out. When I took him to the mayor's office from the cool humid cellar, it was like entering the Sahara. Or a baker's oven, which burns all day. In the fireplace there were far too many logs, but the heat didn't blunt their appetite. I found them both with their mouths full, even though they were a breathless red. I gave a military salute. They lifted their glasses a little higher in return. I wondered, What kind of place is this?'

The little Breton came out of his torpor when he caught sight of the two lawgivers again. He started moaning and then took up his litany of disbelief as before. This put a crimp in Mierck's good mood, so, offhandedly, between two mouthfuls of potted meat, he told him without an extraneous word about the typographer's death. It was news to the little Breton — as well as to Despiaux, for that matter — and the kid took it like a rock to the head. Despiaux had to prop him up.

'You see,' the colonel said, 'your accomplice couldn't live with what you two did.'

'He, at least, had some honour,' added the judge. 'Why don't you make a clean breast of it?'

* * *

There was a silence, but not for long. Despiaux said the kid looked at him and the other two one by one, and then, as if having concluded there was no reasoning with them, he let out a howl — a sound, it seems, no one had ever heard before. Despiaux said he would never have believed a human being could make such a sound, and it went on and on until it was silenced by the sting of the colonel's crop, lashed straight across his cheek. He'd got up deliberately for that. The little Breton was stunned. A purple welt crossed his face, and drops of blood oozed from it slowly. With a jerk of the head, Mierck let Despiaux know he could take him back down to the cellar.

'I've got a better idea,' Matziev said. 'Take him out to the courtyard to jog his memory.'

'To the courtyard?' said Despiaux.

'Yes,' Matziev said, looking out of the window. 'I see there's even a sort of post out there to tie him to. Get on with it!'

'Colonel, sir, it's cold, even freezing — ' Despiaux ventured.

'Do as you're told!' The judge cut him short, tugging a piece of ham from the shank bone.

★ ★ ★

'I was only twenty-two,' Despiaux told me, over a second round of Pernod. 'At twenty-two, what can you say, what can you do? I took the little guy out to the courtyard and tied him to the chestnut tree. It must have been about nine o'clock. We'd left the Sahara of the office and entered the Arctic of the courtyard: it was minus ten degrees, minus twelve maybe. I wasn't proud of myself. 'You'd be better off telling everything if it's you. Then at least you could go back where it's warm,' I whispered in his ear. 'But it's not me, it's not me,' he swore in a low voice. There were dozens of stars in the sky, but the whole courtyard was black. The only light was from the mayor's office, so our eyes were drawn to it. Through the window, it was an unreal scene, like the cut-out of a children's theatre: two men with flushed faces eating and drinking without a care in the world.

186

'I returned to the office, and the colonel told me to wait in the room next door. There I sat down on a sort of bench, waiting and wringing my hands. There was a window in that room too, and from it you could see the courtyard and the prisoner tied to the tree. I stayed in the dark. I didn't want to turn on the light and let him see me. I wanted to run, to get the hell out of there, but respect for the uniform kept me from doing it. Nowadays, that wouldn't keep me from doing anything, believe me! From time to time I heard their voices or the steps of the mayor's servant, who kept bringing them steaming dishes that should have smelled very good. But that day those aromas were like a terrible stink I couldn't get out of my nose. My stomach churned. I never felt such regret to be human.'

★   ★   ★

Louisette made many journeys to and fro. 'It was brass monkey cold!' she tells me. The meal went on for hours. Mierck and Matziev were in no rush, and the alcohol lubricated their revels as one story glided almost without break to another. Louisette hardly looked at them as she served. It was her habit more than it was a judgement. Always kept her eyes on her feet. She never saw the little Breton in the courtyard either. Sometimes it helps matters not to see.

★ ★ ★

Towards midnight, Mierck and Matziev, their lips still glistening from the aspic of the pigs' trotters, were finishing the cheeses. They spoke louder and louder, sometimes breaking into song. Pounded on the table. They had drunk maybe six bottles. Not less, anyway.

They went out to the courtyard, as if for a bit of air. It was the first time Mierck had got near the prisoner since having put him out. For Matziev, who'd been going out between courses, to check on him, it was the fifth visit. They strolled around oblivious to the little Breton's shivering and shuddering. Mierck lifted his head to the clear sky and spoke about the stars. He pointed them all out by name to Matziev. Stars were among the judge's passions. 'They console us human beings, they're so pure.' Despiaux from his darkened window heard those very words. Matziev took out a cigar; he offered one to the judge, who declined courteously. The two of them held forth a while longer on the stars, the moon, the movement of the planets, their heads turning towards the faraway vault.

Then, as though pricked by something sharp, they got around to the prisoner.

For three hours now he'd been out in the cold. He'd had all the time in the world to count those stars, until his tears had nearly frozen.

The colonel passed the burning end of the cigar under his nose several times, asking him the same question over and over. But the little Breton was no longer speaking, only moaning, and after a while this enraged the colonel.

'Are you a man or an animal?' he shouted in his ear, but to no effect. Casting his cigar into the snow, Matziev seized the prisoner, who was still tied to the tree, and shook him violently. Mierck watched the show with fascination, blowing on his fingers. When Matziev had tired of shaking the little Breton's shivering body, he looked all around as though trying to find something. What he found was an idea, a fine son-of-a-bitch idea.

He drew from his pocket a hunting knife, which he used to pop all the buttons off the little Breton's jacket, one by one, methodically, and likewise the ones on his shirt; then with a single stroke he split his undershirt. Once Matziev had stripped the torso, he did the same with the trousers, the long johns, and the underpants. Slicing through the laces, he slowly loosened the boots, whistling 'Caroline and her Patent-Leather Shoes'. The kid was yelling like a madman. Matziev stood up straight again. The prisoner was completely naked at his feet.

'There, perhaps that will clear your head.'

He turned towards the judge, who said, 'Let's go back in, I'm getting cold.'

They shared a chuckle before returning to share the big steaming apple crêpe that Louisette had just laid on the table, along with coffee and a bottle of mirabelle brandy.

★   ★   ★

Despiaux gazed at the June sky, breathing in its softness. The night edged closer. Apart from calling the waiter so our glasses would never be empty, I did nothing but listen. There were a lot of people, frivolous and merry, around our table outside the café; but I really believe we were alone, and I felt cold.

Despiaux told me how the young man had curled up like a dog at the foot of the tree. He could not bear either to watch him or to look away from him, especially when the howls resumed and sounded to Despiaux like what the old folks told of having heard back in the days when we still had wolves in our forests. The former policeman could not contain his

190

grief even at the memory of the scene.

I can imagine Mierck and Matziev standing with their noses against the windowpane, their rumps turned to the fire, glasses of brandy in their hands, and taking in the same scene as they chatted about hare hunting, astronomy or bookbinding. I'm only imagining this, but I'm probably not far wrong.

What's certain is that a little later Despiaux caught sight of the colonel going out again. He went up to the prisoner and nudged him with the tip of his boot, three times — small kicks in the back and the belly, as you might do to see whether a rabid dog is good and dead. The boy tried to catch the boot — to beg, no doubt — but Matziev pushed him off. The little Breton howled louder than ever when the colonel took a pitcher of water he'd brought from the table and poured it over the kid's chest.

'His voice, his voice, if you'd heard his voice — it wasn't really a voice any longer, and what he said was words thrown together helter-skelter, saying nothing. He was making no sense until the end of this litany when he yelled, yelled out that it was him all along, yes, it was him, he confessed to everything, the crime, all crimes, he had killed, murdered . . . You couldn't stop him.'

★ ★ ★

The colonel summoned Despiaux. The kid
was thrashing about, seeming almost giddy at
unburdening himself at last of this long-
sought-after story: 'It's me, it's me, it's me!'
His skin was blue, marbled with red blotches
here and there; the tips of his fingers and toes
had already started turning black with
frostbite. He had the white face of someone
soon to be a corpse. Despiaux wrapped him
in a blanket and helped him walk inside.
Matziev and Mierck raised a glass to their
success. The cold had got the better of the
little Breton. Despiaux couldn't manage to
keep him quiet and listened to him repeating
his story like a schoolboy proud to have
memorised his lesson. The policeman gave
him something hot to drink, but the boy
wasn't able to swallow it. All through the
night, rather than keeping watch on him he
kept watch over him. No official duty to
guard him now. He was nothing.

★ ★ ★

June evenings can almost restore your hope
for the earth and for mankind. There are so
many fragrances, coming from the girls and
the trees, the air so beguiling you want to

192

begin everything anew, to rub your eyes and believe that evil is only a dream and pain but a deceit of the soul. No doubt all that partly explains why I suggested to the former policeman that we go somewhere to have supper. He looked at me as though I'd spoken a profanity. Maybe raking over all these ashes had ruined his appetite. To tell the truth I wasn't so hungry either, only afraid we would part too soon. But before I'd had time to order another round, Despiaux got up. He stretched his massive frame and smoothed his jacket with the palms of both hands. Then he straightened his hat and looked me square in the eye — with a slightly caustic glint I'd never seen in him.

'And you,' he said, his voice suddenly stern, 'where were you that night?'

I sat there, dumbfounded. Clémence came very quickly to my side. I looked at her. She was as beautiful as ever, transparent but so beautiful. What could I say? Despiaux was waiting for my answer. He stood before me, his contempt growing as I sat there, looking back at him — and beyond him — into the emptiness where I alone could see Clémence. He pulled his hat down and turned his back on me without saying goodbye. He walked off. He went home to his regrets and left me to mine. No doubt he knew — as I do — that you can live in regrets as in a country.

19

It was Madame de Flers who led me to
Clémence's bedside. I recognised her instantly.
She was from a very old family in V: high
society, like Destinat. Her husband, the major,
had fallen in battle in September 1914. I
remember having had a cruel thought to the
effect that widowhood would suit her like an
evening dress, that she would use it to scale
new heights at the prefect's parties and char-
ity auctions. I can be extremely stupid sometimes,
so harsh, no better than anybody else. For
right away Madame de Flers, forgoing the
luxury of mourning, wanted to make herself
useful. She left her grand house in V and
came to our town, to the hospital.

People said, 'She won't last three days;
she'll faint when she sees the blood and shit.'
But she did last, in spite of the blood and
shit, her boundless goodness and unpreten-
tious mercies making everyone forget her tide
and her fortune. She slept in a maid's room.
Her waking hours, her days and nights, were
spent at the bedside of those slipping towards
death and those crawling back towards life.
For all the slaughter and mutilation, all its

gutting, befouling, crushing destruction, war can also put some things to rights.

Madame de Flers took me by the hand. I let myself be guided by her as she apologised. 'We have no more rooms, no space for anyone.'

We entered an enormous ward, where the air was full of groans and pervaded by a tart smell of pus and fresh dressings. It was the odour of injury, of pain, and of wounds — not that of death, which is more distinct and horrible. There were thirty beds, maybe forty, on each an oblong form that you could see move a little sometimes, disrupting the uniformity of so many men wrapped like mummies. In the centre of the room, four white sheets hung, describing a sort of alcove, light and undulating. That's where Clémence was, surrounded by soldiers who couldn't see her and of whom she was probably unaware.

Madame de Flers pulled back one of the sheets. She lay there facing straight ahead, her eyes shut, her hands peacefully arranged on her chest. She might have seemed a corpse already except for the stately slow breaths that made her chest swell but left her features impassive. There was a chair near the bed. Gently, Madame de Flers seated me. As she laid her hand on Clémence's forehead and stroked it, she said, without looking away,

'The child is fine.' Then she added, 'I'll leave you now; stay as long as you like.' And pulling a sheet aside as they do at the theatre sometimes, she vanished behind that translucent whiteness.

I remained there all night long. I never stopped looking at her, but I didn't dare speak for fear of being overheard by the wounded who flanked her and would take no comfort in the words of a loving husband. I laid my hand on her to take in her warmth and to give her mine as well; that's how I persuaded myself that she felt my presence and would draw strength from it, the strength to return to me. She was beautiful still. Perhaps a little paler than when I had left her the night before, but sweeter as well, as though the deep sleep in which she wandered had dispelled all causes of unrest, all the worries and pains of day. Yes, she was beautiful.

Never will I have known her ugly, wrinkled, and hunched. For all these years I've lived with a woman who's never grown old. My back is bent, I cough and splutter, I'm broken down and wrinkled up, but she remains unwithered. Death has left me that sense at least, which nothing can take away — even if time has robbed me of her face, so that I must struggle to see it again. Now and then, by way of reward or perhaps taunt, I'm granted a glimpse, in the gleams of the wine I drink or the glare of early morning.

All night long the soldier to Clémence's left, hidden by the sheet, made himself present by babbling a story of which I could make neither head nor tail. Sometimes he hummed, sometimes he grew angry, but he was never still. It was not clear whom he was addressing: a pal, a relative, a sweetheart or just himself. A feverish jumble of subjects — the war of course, but also tales about inheritance, meadows to mow, roofs to patch, a wedding feast, drowned cats, trees covered with caterpillars, an embroidered trousseau, a plough, altar boys, a flood, a mattress lent out and never returned, wood to chop. This chatterbox was constantly reshuffling the moments of his life and dealing them out again by the luck of the draw, just the way life dealt them to him, I suppose. From time to time he repeated a name, Albert Jivonal, with a force and clarity such as one might use to answer an officer. I suppose it was his name and that he needed to say it to remind himself whose story this was.

His voice was like the solo instrument in a symphony of the dying — the heavy breather's timpani, the groans of strings tuning up, the wheezing woodwinds of the gassed, the piccolo of a madman's laughter — and, above it all, the song of Jivonal. His song became ours as I watched over Clémence, the two of us enclosed, it seemed, in the forecastle of a gauzy ship, drifting on the river of the dead.

Towards morning Clémence moved a little, unless it was fatigue that produced this mirage. All the same, I believe her face turned towards me. What I'm sure of is that she breathed a deeper, longer breath than she had up till then. Yes, there was this great breath, like a beautiful sigh, as at the end of some long anticipation; breathing this way, you show you expected it and you're very happy it's occurred. I laid my hand on her throat. And with that I knew. It's surprising sometimes how you can know things without ever having learned them. I knew this sigh was the last. It wouldn't be followed by another. I rested my head against hers. Remaining that way, I felt the warmth leave her little by little. I prayed to God and the saints to let me wake from this dream.

Albert Jivonal died shortly after Clémence. I didn't know he was dead until he fell silent. And when his babbling could bother me no more, I hated him. I don't know if it was rational, but I imagined that once he entered into death he would find himself right near her, waiting in some infinite line and seeing her a few metres ahead of him. So, yes, without knowing him, without even ever having seen his face — he'd suffered a chemical burn — I held his death against him. Jealous of a dead man. Wanting to take his place.

The day nurse came by at seven o'clock. She closed Clémence's eyes; oddly, they had opened at the moment of death. I stayed until midmorning. Nobody dared tell me to go. I left of my own accord, later, alone.

* * *

Morning Glory's burial took place at V the week after the murder. I wasn't there. I had my own grief. I've been told the church was overflowing, that there were also more than a hundred people on the square outside, despite the rain. The prosecutor was there, the judge as well, and Matziev. The family, of course: Bourrache; his wife, who had to be held up on either side; and the little girl's two sisters, Aline and Rose, who didn't seem to understand fully or couldn't bear to. There was also her aunt, Adélaïde Siffert, whose chin quavered like a ewe's and who kept repeating all the way to the cemetery, 'If I had known . . . if I had known . . . ' Of course, you never do.

As for us, there weren't many at the

church. I say us because it seemed to me we still had only each other, even if I was standing and Clémence was lying in the oak coffin flanked by large candles, so I couldn't see or feel her any longer. Father Lurant celebrated the mass. He added words of his own that were simple and right. Under his vestments, I could still see the man in underpants with whom I'd shared a meal and a room as Clémence was dying.

I'd been on bad terms with my father for a long time, and Clémence had no relatives left. It was just as well. I couldn't have stood any of their embraces or pity. I wanted to be alone immediately, having understood that from this time on my life would be that way.

We were six at the graveside: the priest, Ostrane the sexton, Clémentine Hussard, Léocadie Renaut, Marguerite Bonsergent — three old ladies who went to every burial — and me. Everybody listened with head bowed as Father Lurant read the final prayer. Ostrane rested his calloused hands on the handle of his shovel. I was looking at the landscape, the meadows that stretched towards the Guerlante, the hill with its bare trees and dirty brown paths, the congested sky. The old ladies each threw a pathetic flower on the coffin. The priest made the sign of the cross. Ostrane started shovelling in the dirt. I was first to leave. I didn't want to watch.

The following night I had a dream. Clémence was in the ground, crying my name. Sand and roots filled her mouth, and her eyes no longer had pupils. They were blank and lifeless.

I woke up with a start, drenched, panting. Then I saw that I was alone in the bed. It had seemed such a small bed before. I thought of Clémence down there under the ground, on this her first night of exile, and for the first time since she died I cried like a child.

After that there were days — how many, I couldn't say. And nights. I no longer went out. I resolved and then wavered. I would take down Gachentard's rifle, put a round in the magazine, and stick the barrel in my mouth. It's a miracle I lived to play this game so many days, when I was drunk from dawn to dusk. The house looked like a boar's wallow and smelled of the grave. I drew my only strength from wine and brandy. At times I shouted and banged on the walls. Some neighbours came to visit, but their sympathy dried up when I started throwing them out. And then one morning, when I'd scared myself with the sight of my castaway's face in the mirror, a nun from the hospital appeared at the door. In her arms she carried a little bundle of wool that stirred feebly. But that I'll recount a bit later, not right now. I'll tell about it once I've finished with the others.

20

Mierck had jailed the little Breton in the prison of V, though the army was adamant about intending to shoot him. In fact it was a bit of a contest as to who would do the honours. Naturally, this took some time to sort out, time enough for me to have developed a case of cabin fever to compound my desolation and to decide I had to return to work.

When I went to the prison to see him, he'd been there for six weeks. I knew the place. It was a former monastery that dated from the Middle Ages. The prison inmates had simply replaced the monks. Other than that, it hadn't changed much. The refectory was still the refectory; the cells were still the cells. All they'd done was add some bars, heavy doors with strong locks, metal stakes bristling with barbs atop the walls. Light had a hard time penetrating this big building. It was always dark inside, even on the sunniest days. You lost sense of day and night, which was perhaps helpful to the souls of monks, but for the layman this gloomy sameness caused an anxious yearning to leave as soon as you entered. That option was not available to the prisoners, of course.

I told them it was the judge who'd sent me. Not true, but nobody questioned it. They all knew me.

When the guard opened the little Breton's cell door, I couldn't see much of anything. I heard him, though. He was singing very softly in a childish voice — rather pretty, I might add. The guard left me there. As my eyes adjusted to the obscurity, I made him out: he was crouched in a corner, his knees pulled up under his chin, his head rocking constantly to the cadence of his song. He looked younger than his age, less the farm boy I expected than a youth from an ancient myth, with his beautiful blond hair and the blue eyes one could see only when he could bear to take them off the floor. I don't know if he'd heard me come in. Anyway, when I spoke he didn't seem surprised.

'You killed the little girl?' I asked.

He interrupted his song and sang to the same gay tune, without lifting his eyes, 'It was me, it was really me, it was me, it was really me . . .'

'I'm not here on behalf of the judge or the colonel,' I said. 'You don't need to be afraid.'

He looked at me then with the absent smile of one who, having made his choice at a fork in the road, has continued too long to turn back. He was still moving his head like those cherubs in créches, the ones who, when you insert a coin, bob their heads in perpetual thanks. Without adding anything more, he resumed his country ditty of ripe wheat, larks, and wedding bouquets.

I stayed a while longer to consider him, to look at his hands especially. Were these the hands of a strangler? When I left he didn't turn his head but went on singing and rocking. A month and a half later, he would appear before a military tribunal to face the charges of desertion and murder. He was found guilty on both counts and shot forthwith.

The Case was closed.

★ ★ ★

In a single night, Mierck and Matziev had succeeded in turning a simple little peasant into a half-mad confessed killer. Of course, I heard about the events of that night only later, when I finally found Despiaux and induced him to vomit them up. At the time I knew only that neither the judge nor the colonel had gone to question the prosecutor. What Joséphine had said was completely forgotten. In a way it puzzles me to this day.

205

After all, Mierck loathed Destinat, no bones about it! Here was a heaven-sent opportunity to draw blood: at the very least, to drag his name through the gutter and knock him off the pedestal on which he posed like a Roman emperor.

But I suppose the world turns by reason of things stronger than hate. It has its rules, and in the end these matter more than any man's feelings. Destinat and Mierck belonged to the same order of being: good birth, hand-kissing, and motorcars. Above individual particulars and moods, higher even than the laws that men make, there is this code of genteel connivance, this polite tit for tat: 'Don't bother me, and I won't bother you.' To believe that one of your own could be a murderer would be to believe you could be one yourself. And before you know it, all those you've wrinkled your nose at and looked down on as chicken shit, this rabble you've spent your life eyeing with contempt, see that you have a rotten soul just like other men. It's unbearable to contemplate.

And anyway, why should Destinat have killed Morning Glory?

According to the official report, when they arrested the little Breton they'd found in his pocket a five-franc note, with a cross in lead pencil in the upper left corner. Adélaïde

Siffert formally identified it as the note she'd given to her goddaughter that lamentable Sunday. It was a quirk of hers to put crosses on bills, her way of marking them as her own, and — who knows — perhaps to reconcile God and Mammon.

The deserter swore he'd found it along the bank of the little canal. So in fact, he'd gone by there! Yes, but so what? What does that prove? That was also where, under the Blood Sausage — the well-known paint-daubed bridge — he and the typographer had slept, sheltering from the cold and the snow, huddled together: The police had seen the flattened grass and the shape of two bodies. That too he readily confessed.

★　★　★

On the other side of the little canal, almost opposite the small door that leads to the park of the château, stands the factory laboratory. Very long and low, the building looks like a large glass arcade and was lit up night and day, night and day, because the factory never stopped: The laboratory was constantly manned by two engineers, who checked the tolerances and quality of everything that issued from the big monster's gut.

When I asked to speak with the ones who'd

been on duty the night of the crime, Arsène Meyer, head of personnel, looked at the pencil in his hand, turning it every which way.

'Well?' I said, pulling no punches. We'd known each other long enough; besides, he sort of owed me one: I'd turned a blind eye in 1915 when his ne'er-do-well eldest son had got it into his head to help himself to various army supplies — blankets, mess kits, and rations — stored in the warehouses near place de la Liberté. After I had given him a good fright, the prick put everything back and I didn't file a report. Nobody had noticed anyway.

'They're no longer with us,' Meyer tells me.

'No longer with us — since when?'

I could barely hear his reply.

'They went off to England about two months ago.'

England, especially in wartime, might as well have been the ends of the earth. And two months ago: that would have been shortly after the murder.

'Why'd they leave?'

'They were told to.'

'Who told them to?'

'The director.'

'Was this expected?'

Meyer was now sweating as if he'd

committed a crime himself.

'You'd better be on your way,' he said. 'I've got orders. You may be the police, but you're small fry alongside the ones I answer to.'

He'd said what he would, and there was no point in making him squirm further. I left him to his embarrassment, with the intention of putting the question to the director himself the following day.

But my time ran out. My mistake: I should have known the clock was ticking. The next morning at dawn a message arrived: the judge, summoning me to come at once.

As usual, Crusty welcomed me to the antechamber, where I was left to twiddle my thumbs for the obligatory hour. Beyond the leather-tufted door I heard voices — cheerful, or so it seemed to me. When Crusty returned to tell me His Honour the Judge would receive me now, I was busy peeling off a patch of red silk that had come unstuck from the wall. I'd pulled off forty centimetres or more, which I'd then proceeded to shred into a fringe. I thought he might complain, but the clerk just stared at me in sadness, as though at a very sick child, and said nothing.

Mierck was tilting far back in his armchair. Matziev was right beside him like a good soulmate, though a taller, thinner one. It seemed these two had fallen in love with each other: they were never seen apart. Matziev had extended his stay. He still lived at Bassepin's house, driving us crazy with his phonograph. Not until the end of February would he be out of our lives for good.

Charging ahead, Mierck started in on me.

'By what right did you go to the factory?' he barked.

I didn't answer.

'What are you after? The Case has been solved. The guilty have paid the ultimate price.'

'That is officially true, Your Honour,' I said, inflaming him all the more.

'You have some unofficial truth to add?'

'My job is only to make sure there isn't one.'

Matziev fiddled with a cigar that, amazingly, he hadn't lit yet. Mierck mounted another attack. He looked like a suckling pig pulled from the sow's tit by his tail. 'Yours is to protect and not disturb decent people. If I am ever informed of your troubling anyone, anyone at all, about this case, any case we have closed, you can expect to be looking for another way to serve the public.' Having delivered his threat, he rose to stand beside me, almost purring into my ear in a far gentler tone. 'I can understand that you haven't quite been yourself. The loss of your wife — who among us could bear it?'

To hear him speak of Clémence, evoking her memory, took me unawares. It was as if jasmine had just sprouted out of a pile of dung.

'Shut up,' I said.

His eyes widened, he turned purple and he snapped back furiously: 'What! You dare to give me orders? *You?*'

'Go screw yourself,' I replied.

Mierck fell back into his chair, almost breaking it. Matziev looked me up and down and said nothing; he lit his cigar and then went on shaking the match long after it had gone out.

In the street the sun was shining. I felt almost giddy about my unplanned insolence. I really wanted to chat with someone there and then, someone I could trust and who felt as I did about things. I'm not talking about the Case, I'm talking about life and time and such things.

I thought of Mazerulles, the secretary to the education inspector I'd gone to see after Lysia Verhareine was found dead. It would've been nice to see even his turnip head again, his grey complexion, his moist eyes like those of a dog waiting for the hand that was sure to pet it. I started heading towards the place des Carmes, where the inspector's headquarters was. I took my time. No doubt Mierck was already busy demanding my head. But until I received word, I could at least enjoy the memory of unplanned insolence, and the look it had left on Mierck's fat mug.

When I asked the concierge if Mazerulles still worked there, he pushed his glasses up his nose. 'Monsieur Mazerulles left us a year ago,' he told me.

'Is he still in V?'

The guy looked at me as though I'd just arrived from the moon. 'I doubt he could have gone far, but you can always check. He's in the graveyard.'

21

The weeks flew by, and spring returned. Twice a day without fail I would visit Clémence's grave, in the morning and just before evening. I would recount for her the hours of my life as though she were still next to me; I spoke to her in chatty, everyday language — the kind in which words of love don't need grand flourishes and fancy phrases to twinkle like *louis d'or*.

I'd thought about abandoning everything — my job, the house — and moving on. But I remembered that the earth is round, and that soon enough I'd retrace my steps — pretty pointless, all in all. I'd sort of counted on Mierck to send me packing. I told myself he'd surely find a way to have me transferred or suspended. In fact, I was a coward. I foisted off on someone else responsibility for action I couldn't take myself. But Mierck did nothing — nothing that worked, anyway.

Now it was 1918. You could sense the war was about to end. It's easy to write this today, knowing the war really did end in that year, but I don't think I'm lying when I say you could sense it. The feeling made the last convoys of wounded and dead passing through our town seem even more horrible and futile. Our streets were still full of cripples and awful faces, crudely stitched back together. The hospital was always full, like those prestigious seaside resorts that society people recommend to one another. Except that here the high season lasted for four years without slackening. Sometimes I would catch sight of Madame de Flers from a distance, and then my heart would stop — as though she were going to notice me, come to me as she'd done before, and lead me to Clémence's bedside.

Almost every day I walked along the bank of the little canal, where I could continue to root around like a dumb stubborn dog, less to find a crucial detail than to keep things from being forgotten. Often I would make out Destinat's tall figure beyond the wall encircling the park, and I could tell he took note of my pottering there. Since his retirement he hardly left the château, except for the occasional trip to V, and received even less frequently — that is to say, he didn't receive a soul. He spent his days in silence, said Barbe, not even reading, seated at his desk with folded hands, gazing out the window. Or else he would stroll in his park, like a lone animal. At bottom, we weren't all that different, he and I.

One day — it was June 13 that same year — as I was walking along the bank, I heard grass rustling behind me just past the Blood Sausage. I turned around to find Destinat. He was even taller than in my memory, his grey mane still lustrous but almost white, smoothed back from his forehead. He wore a black suit, and his shoes were impeccably polished as ever; a small ivory knob topped the cane in his right hand. He looked at me without stepping forwards. I think he was waiting for me to pass before he would come out through the door at the edge of his park.

We eyed each other without speaking, like two old rams.

Destinat spoke first. 'I see you here often, you know . . . '

He dragged the sentence out without trying to finish it, or without being able to. For my part, I didn't know what to say. It had been so long since I'd addressed him, I couldn't remember how it was done.

With the tip of his cane, he dug into the moss that bordered the bank. Coming a little closer, he scrutinised me — not maliciously but with an unwholesome precision. The strange thing was that his gaze didn't embarrass me; rather, it gave me a feeling of bliss, soothing and calm, as when an old doctor we've known since childhood examines us to get to the bottom of our aches and pains.

'You never came to ask me . . . '

Here again he didn't end his sentence. I saw his lips quiver slightly, and his eyes seemed troubled by the glare. I knew what he wanted to talk about. We understood each other quite well.

'Would I have had an answer?' I asked, dragging out my words as he did.

He breathed deeply. With his left hand he fished out his watch; it hung from the end of a chain, to the other end of which an odd little black key was also attached. Then he gazed into the distance, at the beautiful pale blue sky, but quickly his eyes came to rest on me once more and now their penetration made me flinch.

'We should be wary of answers — they're never what we want them to be, don't you think?'

With the tip of his left boot he nudged into the water the bit of moss he'd dislodged with his cane. New moss of a tender green, it waltzed around in an eddy before heading midstream where it sank.

When I looked up, Destinat had gone.

★   ★   ★

Life picked up again, as they say, with the end of the war. The hospital gradually emptied; so did our streets. The cafés did less business; so did Agathe Blachart, who had not yet left for Australia. Sons came home, husbands too: some still whole, others badly damaged. Of course, many never reappeared; but despite all proof to the contrary, there were those who held out hopes of seeing them turn the corner, come into the house, and sit down at the table, expecting their pitcher of wine. As these families emerged from the terrible years, others, whose menfolk worked at the factory and who had gone through the war without much worry or privation, were paying the price of their good luck. Between these opposing camps the rift grew ever deeper. Some wouldn't speak to those across the divide. Others had reached the point of unveiled hatred.

Bassepin launched his monument business. In fact, one of the first he furnished was for our town: a soldier with the flag in one hand and a rifle in the other, his body lurching awkwardly forwards on a slightly bent knee. Beside him was a French cockerel, huge and bursting with pride, portrayed at the moment when he belts out his song, tilted upward on his spurs.

The mayor unveiled it on 11 November,

1920. He made a speech — quavers, flights of fancy, rolling eyes — and then read out the names of the forty-three from our town who'd died for their country; after each name he paused for Aimé Lachepot, the local policeman, to give a solemn drumroll. Women in black wept; their children, those still small and heedless, took them by the hand and tried to drag them to Margot Gagneure's store close by, especially for the liquorice sticks and honey lollipops.

Then there was the raising of the colours. The band played a dirge that brought everyone to their feet, standing up straight with an unswerving gaze, and after the last measure was finished, one and all rushed to the town hall, where a reception was held. People talked. They even started laughing again. The dead were forgotten over sparkling wine and pâté on toast. The living parted an hour later, ready to re-enact year after year this sham of heavy hearts and remembrance.

Destinat was at the ceremony, in the front row; I was two metres behind him. But he didn't come to the town hall. Slowly, he made his way back to the château.

Though he'd been retired for more than four years, there were, as I've said, the occasional trips to V. Solemn would have the horses harnessed by ten minutes to ten. At ten on the dot, Destinat would come down and settle into the carriage, and away they'd go. Once in town, he walked through the streets. It was always the same route: rue Marville, place de la Préfecture, allée Baptiste-Villemaux, rue Plassis, rue d'Autun, place Fidon, rue des Bourelles. Solemn followed in the carriage twenty metres behind, stroking both horses with his hand to calm them; they tended to pound the ground with their hooves while dropping their loads of dung. Destinat would be greeted by people of the city. He nodded slightly, never exchanging a word.

At noon he would enter the Rébillon, where Bourrache welcomed him as always. He still had his table. Without fail, he ate the same dishes and drank the same wine as when he'd made heads roll. The difference was that now he lingered after his coffee. The dining room would empty, but Destinat remained. Then he would wave Bourrache over to join him. The innkeeper would pick up a bottle of brandy — one of his best — along with two little glasses and sit down across from the prosecutor. He would fill the glasses, gulping his down. As for Destinat, he whiffed the alcohol but never brought it to his lips.

Then the two would talk.

'About what?' I dared to ask Bourrache one day, though only after many years had gone by.

His gaze lost its focus. You would have thought he was looking at a distant scene or through a stranger's glasses. His eyes began to glisten.

'About my little girl,' he said, and big tears rolled down the stubble on his cheeks. 'It was mainly the prosecutor who talked at first, and I who listened. Such a pleasure to listen to a man of intelligence and learning. Nothing escaped his notice. Belle had hardly said a word to him when she brought his bread or a carafe of water, but he apprehended everything about her. He could bring her to life in a way I could not in my own memories. He would paint a picture for me, speak about her complexion, her hair, her birdlike voice, the shape of her mouth, and its colour as well. He would mention the names of painters I didn't know and say she could have been in their pictures. And then he would ask every question you can imagine — about her character, her little quirks, her childish sayings, her sicknesses, her earliest years. He let me talk, on and on and on, and he never wearied.

'And every time he came back, it was the same: 'What if we spoke about her now, my dear Bourrache,' he would begin. As for me, my heart wasn't in it. I was filled with grief, and the feeling would last all through the end of the day and into the evening too. But I could hardly be rude to the prosecutor, so I would talk too. An hour, two hours — I think he would've been happy to let me continue for days on end. It must have been his age, poor fellow. I suppose he was getting a bit senile and took an old man's pleasure in hearing the same story over and over. And being all alone, never having had a child of his own, that must have been gnawing at his mind.

'One day he even asked me for a photograph of my little girl. Can you imagine? Photographs are so expensive, we hardly ever made any. I had only three; one of them showed my three daughters. Belle's godmother had insisted on paying for it. She'd taken them to Isidore Kopieck, the Russian in the rue des États. He posed them with the two older girls sitting on the floor, against a setting of grass and flowers, and Belle standing between them, her smile full of grace like the Blessed Virgin's. I had three copies, one for each girl, so I gave Belle's copy to the prosecutor. It's not often common folk have a chance to be generous to grand people. His gratitude could not have been more profound. He almost tore my arm off, pumping my hand in thanks.

'It was a week before his death, the last time he came in. The same ritual as always: the meal, the coffee, the brandy, the conversation. The same questions about my poor little girl, nearly always the same. Then, after a long silence, he told me almost in a murmur, in the tone of wise pronouncement, 'She never knew evil; she left us without knowing it; but as for the rest of us, evil has marked us forever.' Then he got up slowly and gave me a long fond handshake. I helped him on with his coat, and he picked up his hat. He looked intently around the empty room, the tables waiting for the next seating. I should have known when I opened the door and said, 'See you next time, Mr Prosecutor.' He smiled without answering, as everyone else knew him to do.'

★ ★ ★

Poor Bourrache. The pain of remembering. Writing brings it upon me. I know this, now that I've been at it for months. It's a pain in your hand but also in your soul. Man wasn't meant to do this — and what's the point, anyway? What's the point for me? If Clémence hadn't left, I would never have scribbled all these pages — despite Morning Glory's death and all its mystery, despite the little Breton's death and the blot it left on my conscience. Yes, just her presence would have given me the strength to leave the past behind and not look back. But now I have nowhere to go and no means of travel. And so I write to trick myself, to pretend, to convince myself she's still waiting for me, waiting to hear from me, wherever she may be. My words speak and she listens.

Writing makes me live for two, when I cannot live for one.

Living alone a long while, one must do something. Most people wind up talking to the walls. I've often wondered what the prosecutor chose to do. How did he spend his hours? Who was it he devoted his little thoughts to, his inner conversations? In the end, only a widower understands a widower, or so it seems to me. All in all, many things could have brought us closer.

22

On 27 September, 1921, as I was crossing the rue du Pressoir, I was knocked down by an automobile I hadn't seen coming. I remember the moment my forehead hit the kerb. I thought of Clémence and, believing she was still alive, imagined them informing her that her husband had been in an accident. In that same fraction of a second I kicked myself for being so scatterbrained as not to have looked before crossing; it was my fault she would have to endure this trauma. Then I fainted, almost happily, as though I'd been led into a lovely quiet pasture. When I awoke at the hospital, they told me I'd drifted in this strange sleep for seven days. Seven days away from my life, so to speak, seven days of which I have no memory at all. In fact, the doctors thought I would never wake up. They were wrong. I had no luck.

'We came very close to losing you!' one of them told me when I awoke: a cheerful young man with wide brown eyes, young enough not to have lost every illusion of youth over the past few years. I made no reply. In that great night I hadn't found Clémence. I hadn't heard or sensed her presence. So, contrary to professional opinion, I must in fact have been a long way from dying.

They kept me for two more weeks. I was strangely weak. I knew none of the nurses who cared for me, but they seemed to know me. They brought me soups, herbal teas, boiled meat. I kept looking for Madame de Flers. I even asked one of them if she was still there. The nurse smiled without answering. She must have thought I was delirious.

When they decided I was strong enough, I had a visit from the mayor. He shook my hand. Told me I'd had a close call; he'd fretted about it an awful lot. Then he dug into his baggy trousers and fished out a package of sticky candies. He laid them on the night table somewhat sheepishly. 'I wanted to bring you a nice bottle of wine, but they have their rules here, so I said to myself — well, anyway, the confectioner fills these with plum brandy.'

He laughed. I laughed too, to put him at ease. I wanted to talk, to ask him questions; but he raised his finger to his lips, as if to say there would be time enough for that. The nurses had warned him not to overtax me. We continued the visit this way a few moments, looking at each other, looking at the candy, the ceiling, the window through which you could see nothing but a slice of sky, not a tree or a hill or a cloud.

When the mayor got up to go, he shook my hand again, deliberately. He didn't inform me that day of Destinat's death. I would hear about it two days later from Father Lurant, when he came to visit me.

It had happened the day after my accident. He died as simply as could be, without fuss or theatre — at home on a beautiful autumn day, golden and red and just barely cool, the memory of summer still hanging in the air.

He'd gone out as every day for a mid-afternoon stroll in the park of the château; and at the end of his walk he'd sat down as usual on the bench overlooking the Guerlante, his hands folded across the top of his cane. Normally he would have stayed there like that for a little under an hour and then gone back in.

On that day, when she didn't see him return, Barbe grew worried and went out into the park; when she caught sight of him in the distance, still sitting on the bench with his back to her, she felt reassured and tended to her kitchen again, where she was cooking a joint of veal. But once her roast was done, and the vegetables for the soup had all been peeled, chopped, and put into a pot, it occurred to her that she still hadn't heard the prosecutor's steps. She went out again and saw him still seated on his bench, seemingly indifferent to the fog rising from the river, to the night gradually enveloping all the trees, and to the swarm of squabbling crows in the branches. Barbe crossed the park, to tell her master supper would be ready soon, but when she called to him she got no reply. By the time she'd drawn close, only a few metres away, she had a sinking presentiment. Walking slowly, she circled around in front of the bench to find Destinat sitting upright, his eyes still open wide, his hands folded on the knob of his cane.

It's said that life is unfair, but death is even more so — the business of dying, in any case. There's no sense to who suffers and who passes without a sigh. Justice is not of this world, but it's not of the other one either. Destinat had passed away without pain or murmur — and without warning. He went all alone, just as he had lived.

Father Lurant said the funeral was worthy of a minister, with every show of beauty and pomp our region could muster. The gentlemen were dressed in black tailcoats and the women in sombre tones, their faces obscured by grey veils. The bishop had taken the trouble to come, as well as the prefect and an undersecretary of state. When the cortege reached the cemetery, a eulogy was delivered by Destinat's successor in office. Then Ostrane did his part, lending his shovel and his eccentricity.

As soon as I got out of the hospital, before returning home, I went to the cemetery to see Clémence and to see him. I walked very slowly, with a stiffness in my left leg that has never left me; it gives me the gait of a veteran, though I never fought a war.

I sat on the slab over Clémence's grave, and I told her about my accident: my fear of causing her grief, my long pleasant sleep, my disappointment at waking up. I cleaned the marble and pulled up the clover growing along the stone; with the palm of my hand, I rubbed away the lichens that blistered the cross. Then I blew her a kiss through the air, with its wholesome scent of humus and damp meadow.

Destinat's grave was hidden under wreaths of flowers and beads. The flowers had almost rotted away, and their rusty petals were scattered on the surrounding gravel path. The beads glistened and, catching a ray of sun now and then, seemed for that moment like diamonds. There were also sagging bouquets, muddied ribbons, ornate plaques, and visiting cards in envelopes that remained unopened. I said to myself that for him it was done; at last he was with his wife. He'd taken his time about it. A lifetime. I thought about his tall figure, his silence, his mystery, that aura of solemnity and distance that emanated from his being — and I wondered if I was standing before the grave of a murderer.

23

Several years later, after Barbe's funeral, I told myself it was time for me to enter the château. The key she had given me made me lord of an abandoned domain. When I walked from the cemetery to the great mansion I made my way haltingly, as if towards something long awaiting me that I hadn't dared to see.

Turning that key in the tall door, I imagined myself unsealing an envelope that held thin paper — on which, in pale letters, the whole truth had always been inscribed from the first. And I'm not just speaking of the truth about the Case; I'm speaking of my own truth, of what made me this man I am, a man drifting through life.

While the prosecutor was alive, I had never set foot in the château. It was no place for me. A dishcloth among silk handkerchiefs, that's how I would have felt. I had been content to brush by, to glimpse it from afar at sunset in its continuous blaze, its vast fire of high slates and copper gables. And then there had been Lysia Verhareine's death, Destinat waiting for me at the top of the steps before the door with a frightened air, and the two of us trudging towards the little house like convicts in a chain gang, climbing the stairs to her room.

The château wasn't a dead man's abode. It was an empty place — or, rather, *emptied* — emptied of its life long before. That the prosecutor had lived there, that Barbe had, and Solemn too, didn't matter one whit: vacancy could be felt before you crossed the threshold. The château was itself deceased, having stopped breathing ages ago, stopped resounding with the sound of steps, of voices, of laughter, of murmurs, of arguments, of dreams, and of sighs.

Inside, it wasn't cold. There was no dust, no spiderwebs, none of the debris you expect to send tumbling when you force the locks of tombs. In the hall with its black-and-white draughtboard tiles, it seemed robbers had taken the pieces. There were vases, majestic pedestal tables, and gilded consoles on which dancing couples, frozen in Saxe porcelain, had suspended the movements of their minuet for centuries. In the huge mirror that offered the visitor his reflection, I discovered I was fatter, older, and uglier than I had imagined: I was facing a distorted image of my father, a grotesque resurrection.

In a corner a big faïence dog stood guard,

its jaws gaping, its fangs of glittering enamel, its tongue thick and red. From the ceiling, so high it was barely visible, hung a chandelier that surely weighed three tons, a realisation that heightened the unease of anyone standing beneath it. On the wall opposite the door was a large portrait in shades of cream, silver, and blue, a very young woman in a long dress and a diadem of pearls. Her complexion was pale despite the darkening of the varnish over the years, her mouth the slightest mark of pink, her eyes dreadfully melancholy though she forced herself to smile. She held herself elegantly erect, but you could sense a poignant resignation. With one hand she was opening a fan of lace and mother-of-pearl, while the other rested on a stone lion's head.

I lingered many minutes gazing at this woman I'd never seen, this woman I'd never known: Clélis de Vincey . . . Clélis Destinat. She'd been mistress of the house, after all, and so quite entitled to look her oafish visitor up and down. In fact the thought almost had me turning around to get the hell out of there. What right did I have to come and stir up the still air, jostle its ghosts?

But the figure in the portrait seemed perfectly benevolent, if a bit surprised. I think I spoke to her. I don't know exactly what I said; that's hardly important. She was a dead woman from another time. Her attire, her coiffure, her manner, her pose — it all made her seem a kind of sumptuous if brittle museum display. And I could have seen her that way, like the large faïence dog, had her face not reminded me of so many others, dancing in a circle, in motion and fleeting, their blurred features in constant flux, now ageing, now growing younger; such was the swirl that I never managed to pin down one face or the other, to look at it long enough to see who it was.

I was surprised that the prosecutor had never taken down this painting. I couldn't have lived with so large a picture of Clémence set in front of me like that, every day and every hour. One day I tossed all the pictures of her I had into the fire, those lying photographs in which her bright smile shone. I knew if I had kept them I would have overloaded my sorrow, like an already heavy cart that, if laden with one more burden, would topple into the ditch.

Might it be that, in the end, Destinat couldn't see through this big canvas any longer — that it had become more a beautiful object than a portrait of the wife he'd loved and lost? Could it be that he'd earned that museum visitor's privilege which permits us to look unmoved upon figures under varnishes, hardly believing they ever lived like us, ever breathed, slept, suffered?

The half-drawn blinds lent all the rooms a pleasant shadowing. Everything was in order, tidy and spotless, as if awaiting a master away on vacation who would be back any day now to regain his dominion. The oddest part is that there wasn't a whiff of any scent to be detected. A house without odours is a dead house indeed.

I continued on this peculiar voyage for a long while, a cheeky prowler unwittingly following a well-marked path. The château was a seashell, and as I progressed slowly through its spiral, heading gradually towards its heart, I passed the commonplace rooms — kitchen, pantry, laundry, linen closet, sitting room, dining room, smoking room — till I reached the library, an enveloping cove of beautiful books.

It wasn't very large: There was a desk with a writing set, a hand-warmer lamp, a very ordinary letter opener, and a blotter in black leather. Flanking the desk were two broad deep chairs, with armrests that curved up high. One chair was like new. The other preserved the imprint of a body; the leather was crackled, and shinier in patches as well. I sat down in the new one. It felt comfortable.

Right across from me was the one in which Destinat had spent so many hours, reading or thinking of nothing.

All those books, arranged along the walls in the perfect order of cadets in formation, muffled the sounds from outside. You could hear nothing but your own breath, neither the wind nor the hum of the factory, close as it was, nor the birds in the park. On Destinat's chair a book lay open, splayed upside down on the armrest. It was a very old book, with brittle pages that fingers had turned again and again, no doubt, throughout an entire life. I took the book and have it beside me still: Pascal's *Pensées*. I have it opened to the very page where he had left off. And on that page, cluttered with cloying pieties and addled comments, there are two sentences that shed their light like gold earrings left on a pile of dung, two sentences underlined in pencil by Destinat's hand that I know by heart:

The last act is bloody, however lovely the play may have been up till then. In the end they throw dirt over your head, and that's it forever.

Some words send a shiver down your spine and leave you speechless: those words, for example. I don't know about Pascal's life — and I don't give a damn — but I'm sure he must have been none too pleased with the play he's speaking of. Like me. Like Destinat, no doubt. He too must have drunk from a bitter cup and lost beloved faces all too soon. Otherwise he could never have written that; when you live among the flowers, you don't think about the mud.

With the book in my hand, I went from bedroom to bedroom. There were lots of them, and each resembled the others: bare rooms. What I mean is that they'd always been bare, as if neglected, without memories, without a past, without an echo. They were full of the sadness of objects that have never been of any use. They'd needed a touch of roughhousing, some scuffing up, a fog of breath against their windowpanes, the weight of heavy tired bodies in their four-posters, children's games scattered on their rugs, knocks on their doors, tears fallen on their parquet floors.

At the very end of a hallway was Destinat's room, at some remove from the others, a bit set off on its own, fittingly enough. The door was taller and more austere, a dark colour something like garnet. It could only have been his room, there, at the end of this corridor that was more a gallery, a ceremonial walkway commanding you to take it with a measured gait, solemn and circumspect. On either side there were engravings on the walls: holdovers from rancid centuries, bewigged antique noggins with ruffled necks, thin moustaches, and garlands of Latin inscription. Just to pluck up my courage, I cursed them all as I approached the big door.

Destinat's room was nothing like the others. Muted and cold like him, like him it commanded a certain respect. The bed was small and narrow, made for one and monastic in its simplicity: iron bedposts, a thin mattress, no frills or flounces, no meringue overhanging it. The walls were covered in plain grey cloth, without picture or decoration of any sort. Near the bed, on a small table, lay a crucifix. At the foot of the bed, a grooming set, pitcher, and basin. Opposite where he slept, a desk on which everything had been put away: no book, no paper, no pen.

From the sleep of its occupant the room had drawn the immeasurable reserve that made it scarcely a human place, damned for all eternity to remain impervious to laughter, to joy, to sighs of contentment, its very order a token of deadened hearts.

Still with Pascal's book in my hand, I went to the window: a beautiful view of the Guerlante, the little canal, the bench where death had come for Destinat, the small house in which Lysia Verhareine had lived.

I was as close as possible to what had been Destinat's life. Not his professional one but his inner life, the truth we mask with ingratiation, exertion, politeness, and small talk. His whole universe had been the void of these cold walls, these sparse furnishings. I wouldn't have been surprised, in this room so far from the living, to see a dead man return, to see him suddenly appear and say he'd been waiting for me, wondering at my having taken so long. But the dead have their own business to tend to, which never coincides with ours.

In the drawers of the writing desk, carefully stored, were block calendars from which all the days were torn away, leaving only stubs imprinted with the year. There were dozens of them, attesting to thousands of days gone by, Wasted, tossed in the bin like the slips that had represented them. Destinat had kept the stubs. We keep such rosaries as we can.

The largest drawer was locked. I knew there was no point in looking for that little key, which must have been the black one so oddly shaped. I felt sure it had been taken to the grave, hooked to the end of a chain with the watch at its other end, tucked into the watch pocket of a vest by now perhaps already in tatters.

I forced the drawer with my knife. The wood gave way in a spray of splinters.

There was only a single object inside, and I recognised it right away. I stopped breathing. Everything seemed enchanted. It was the little notebook, rectangular and delicate, bound in fine red morocco, that I'd seen Lysia Verhareine holding in her hands. That had been years ago. It was the day I'd climbed to the crest of the hill and caught her gazing at the vast killing field. Suddenly it seemed to me that she entered the room, laughing only to freeze, surprised once more at my awkward presence.

I snatched the notebook — afraid it would catch fire in my hand — and rushed out like a thief.

I'm not too sure what Clémence would have thought of all that, whether she would have found it good or bad. I know I felt ashamed, the delicate notebook weighing like lead in my pocket.

I ran and ran. And once I had shut myself away in my house, I set about emptying a bottle of brandy until my heart and breath had begun to slow.

I waited till evening with the little notebook on my knees, not daring to open it, looking at it that way for hours, like some living creature I had discovered in the woods. When evening came my head was hot. I had for so long kept my legs squeezed together and immobile I couldn't feel them. I could feel only the note-book, which made me think of a heart I was sure would start beating again when I touched its cover and laid it open. A heart I would break into, a different sort of burglary.

24

13 December, 1914
My darling,
At last I'm near you. This morning I
arrived in P, a town only a few kilometres
from the front where you are. I was
accorded a most charming welcome. The
mayor rushed to greet me as his saviour.
The school is abandoned. I will replace
the teacher there, who's seriously ill, so
I'm told. His lodgings were in a
deplorable state; I'll have to find a place
to settle into. For now I'm going to stay
at a hotel. The mayor took me there.
He's a fat peasant who plays at being a
young blade. You'd find him funny, no
doubt. I miss you so much. But knowing
that you're near me, knowing that we
breathe the same air, see the same clouds,
the same sky — all of that comforts me.
Look after yourself; be very careful. I love
you and kiss you tenderly.
     Your Lyse

16 December, 1914
My darling,

I've settled into a marvellous place, a doll's house in a great park that belongs to a beautiful mansion. People here call it the château. They exaggerate a bit; it's not a real château, but it is charming all the same. The mayor was the one who came up with the idea. We went to see the owner, who's an old widower. He's the prosecutor in V. When we met, he couldn't even bring himself to say hello. He just held my hand a long while, as though surprised to be meeting anyone. Such a deep sadness in his eyes. In the end he gave the mayor his consent, said goodbye to me, and left us.

The little house hasn't been lived in for quite some time. I'll have to do a lot of tidying up. I hope you can see it someday. I miss you so much. For letters, the address is simply Château, rue des Champs-Fleury. Your last one was dated three weeks ago, and too much time has passed without word that you are well. I hope you're not suffering too much on account of this cold weather. We hear gun blasts day and night. My whole being shudders. I'm afraid. I love you and kiss you tenderly.

Your Lyse

23 December, 1914
My darling,
I'm so worried: still no news from you,
and the gun blasts never stop. They said
the war wouldn't last long. If only you
knew how I long for your arms, to be
held in them and see your smile, your
eyes. I can't wait for this war to be over
so I can marry you and have some
beautiful children to tug on your
moustache! Oh, if only our parents
hadn't been so foolish last year, we
would already belong to each other. If
ever you write them, don't tell them
where I am. I left without warning. It
doesn't matter: as far as I'm concerned,
they've ceased to exist.

I'm trying to take my new job
seriously. The children are obedient at
least. In fact, I'm fond of them, and I
think they're fond of me too. Many of
them bring me little gifts — an egg, some
walnuts, a piece of bacon. They give me a
bit of peace and let me forget my
loneliness a little.

Sadness (that's the nickname I've
given to my landlord, the prosecutor)
waits for me every day to come back
home. He strolls in his park, says hello. I
return his greeting and give him a smile.

He can't begin to cope with his loneliness, the housekeeper says. His wife died when they were very young.

Christmas is coming. Remember our last Christmas, how happy we were! Write to me soon, my darling, write to me . . .

I love you and kiss you tenderly.
Your Lyse

7 January, 1915
My darling,
Your letter, at last! It arrived today, though you wrote it on December 26. And to think you are so nearby. Sadness handed it to me in person. He must have suspected the nature of the correspondence when he saw my excitement, but he was discreet. He knocked at my door, said hello, gave me the envelope, and promptly left.

I wept with joy as I read your words. I hold your letter close; yes, I hold it close, I press it to my skin, as though it's you there with your warmth and your scent, when I close my eyes.

I'm so afraid for you. Here we have a hospital where every day the wounded arrive by the truckload. I dread so much that I might see you among them. The poor things are in an inhuman state; some of them don't have faces any more, others moan as though they've lost their minds.

Keep safe, my darling, and think of me. I love you and long to be your wife. I kiss you tenderly.

Your Lyse

23 January, 1915
My darling,
I miss you. I've spent so many months already without seeing you, without talking to you, without touching you. Why on earth can't you get some leave? I'm so very sad. I try to stay cheerful around the children, but sometimes I can feel tears coming to my eyes, and then I turn to the blackboard and write some words so they won't notice anything.

I shouldn't complain. Everybody is nice to me here, and I feel at home in this little house. Sadness still keeps his respectful distance, but he never fails to cross my path at least once a day so he can say hello. I don't know if it was only the cold weather, but yesterday I think he blushed. His old servant Barbe lives there with her husband. She and I get along very well. Sometimes I join her and Solemn — that's her husband's name! — for a meal.

I've got into the habit of climbing to the top of the hill every Sunday. There's a big meadow up there where you can take in the whole horizon. You're just beyond it, my darling; I see the fumes, the horrible explosions. I stay as long as I can, till my hands and feet go numb from the bitter cold; I want to share your suffering. My poor darling. How much longer will this drag on?

I kiss you tenderly. I'm waiting for your letters.

With love,
Your Lyse

25

In the little notebook of red morocco there were many pages like that, covered with fine-spun slanted writing like a delicate frieze, pages on which were composed many letters from Lysia Verhareine to the man she loved and had followed. I could imagine her rewriting them on beautiful vellum before she put out the light.

Bastien Francoeur was his name: twenty-four years of age, corporal in the 27th Infantry. She wrote to him every day. She told him about the long hours, the children's mischief, Destinat's blushes, the presents from Martial Maire — the simpleton for whom she'd become the divinity of the park — the breath of spring that came to plant primroses and crocuses. She told him about all that in her small light hand, in phrases just as light, behind which anyone who'd known her even a bit could detect her smile. Above all she told about her love and her loneliness, that heartbreak she concealed from us so well; though our paths crossed hers every day, we had never suspected a thing.

The notebook didn't contain any letters

from her lover. Besides, she hadn't received very many: nine in eight months. She counted them, of course. She read them again and again. Where did she keep them? Maybe she held them close, close to herself, even pressed to her skin, just as she'd written.

So few letters — why? Not enough quiet time? Or not enough desire? We always know what others mean to us, but we never really know what we mean to them. Was Bastien's love as strong as hers? I'd like to think so, but I couldn't say.

The fact remains that the little teacher lived by this correspondence; her lifeblood flowed into her words. After she'd corrected her pupils' exercise books, the light in the house must have shone late as she took up her pen to write out the letter she'd first composed in the red morocco notebook. Maybe writing them there first answered another need: to create a journal of absence, a book of lonesome days she spent far from the man for whose sake she'd exiled herself among us — a more eloquent form of Destinat's bundles of dutifully preserved stubs.

She mentions Sadness quite often; I believe she was full of affection for the cold lonely man who'd given her a home. While perfectly aware of his pitiful efforts to find favour with her, she noted them with only a tender irony; there was no malice when she described his face turning crimson at times, his stammers, his pompous get-ups, his circuits around the little house, the way he would gaze up at her bedroom window imagining no one saw him. Sadness amused her, and I think I can swear without fear of contradiction that Lysia Verhareine was the only human being in his entire life the prosecutor ever managed to amuse.

As for that improbable meal that had flabbergasted Barbe, the girl described it in a long letter dated 15 April, 1915:

My darling,
Yesterday evening I was invited for the first time to dine with Sadness. Such formality. Three days ago I had found a little card slid under my door: 'Prosecutor Pierre-Ange Destinat requests the pleasure of the company of Mademoiselle Lysia Verhareine for dinner, Wednesday, 14 April, at eight o'clock.' I got myself ready for a dinner in society, but it was only a tête-à-tête with him — just the two of us in an immense dining room that could have seated sixty! A real romantic rendezvous! I'm teasing you! Sadness, as I've told you, is almost an old man. But

yesterday he looked like a minister or a chancellor, standing straight, in tails worthy of an evening at the opera! The table was dazzling, the china, the tablecloth, the silver — I felt like I was in . . . I don't know, Versailles perhaps!

Instead of Barbe, a very young beautiful child served at table. Eight years old, maybe nine. But she took her role very seriously and seemed to know all the ropes. Sometimes she stuck out the tip of her tongue, as children do when they try to apply themselves. Occasionally our eyes met and she smiled at me. It was all rather strange — the dinner for two, the little girl. Barbe told me today that the child — who is called Morning Glory — is the daughter of an innkeeper in V. Her father had prepared the meal. Everything was superb, though one could hardly enjoy it. I don't know when I've seen such a feast — but suddenly I feel ashamed, thinking of you, hunting for a potato and maybe even going hungry! Forgive me, my darling, I'm stupid . . .

I miss you so much. Your last letter was dated six weeks ago. And still no leave. Even so, I know somehow you are safe — I can sense it. Write to me, my darling. Your words give me strength to continue here, just as knowing that you are so close by sustains me, even if I can't see you or hold you in my arms.

Sadness hardly spoke at dinner. I would sometimes look up to catch him looking at me, and he would look away, like a shy adolescent. When I asked him whether his solitude didn't weigh on him too much, he paused for a moment and then he said, softly and solemnly: 'To be alone is the human condition, in any event.' I thought that very beautiful, even knowing it to be untrue: you are not with me, yet I feel your presence every moment. A little before midnight he escorted me to the door, where he said goodnight and kissed my hand. Romantic, but so passé, like an antique gentleman, which I suppose is what he is.

Oh, my darling, how much longer is this war going to last? I'm laying my head down to sleep now. Sometimes when I dream of you, in the morning I can't bear to open my eyes right away and leave the dream for the nightmare that awaits me by day.

Desperate for your embrace, I kiss you with all the force of my love.

Your Lyse

In time, the young teacher's long-unanswered letters turned to bitterness, despondency, and occasionally venom. All we knew of her was the glowing smile and the pleasant, courteous word she had for everyone; underneath, pain and darkness were filling her heart. She began with greater regularity to express disgust at the men in our town, the ones who reported to work at the factory clean and rested. Even the wounded released from the hospital to loiter in our streets did not escape her contempt; she called them *the lucky ones*. Still, I can hardly describe my surprise to have been singled out for special loathing, a distinction I became aware of when I read the letter she'd written the evening of that indelible day when I'd seen her on the crest of the hill, staring at the distant plain as if she could divine from it some meaning.

4 June, 1915
My darling,
Your letters are like old newsprint, I've unfolded them, reread them, and cried over them so often. How I suffer. Time seems like a monster, born to divide lovers. They have no appreciation of how lucky they are, these cows I see every day, separated from their husbands for only a few hours, and these children

whose fathers come home for supper each evening.

Today as every Sunday I climbed to the top of the hill to be closer to you. Up there a great wind brought me the noise of the big guns. They banged and banged and banged. I wept at the thought of you sheltering under that downpour of iron and fire, of which I could see only ominous smoke and flashes. My darling, where were you? Where are you? I stayed there a long time, as usual; I couldn't tear my eyes away from that immense field of suffering where you've lived for months.

Suddenly I sensed a presence behind my back. It was a man I know by sight. He's a policeman, and I've always wondered what on earth he's doing in this little town. He's older than you are but still young and fit. I suppose he's on the right side, the side of the cowards. He was looking at me dumbfounded, carrying a hunting rifle, a ridiculous shiny gun for children or the stage. Can you imagine ambling around with a weapon for idle killing while a few miles away men are slaughtering and being slaughtered with rifles? That moment I hated this comical buffoon more than anything in the world. He mumbled incoherently, and in my disgust I turned my back on him.

I'd gladly send thousands of his sort into the jaws of hell for a few seconds in your arms. I'd sever their heads with my own hands just to taste your kisses again, to touch your hands and look into your eyes. I don't care if I seem horrible. I don't care about judgements, morality, or other people. I would kill to keep you alive. I hate death because it chooses without care.

Write to me, my darling, write to me. Each day without you is a bitter eternity.

Your Lyse

I couldn't hold it against her. She was right. I had acted like a prick on the hilltop, and what was I now, as I read her private thoughts? Would I not have killed to have kept Clémence alive? I found the living no less detestable than Lysia Verhareine did. I bet the prosecutor felt the same. Anyone could tell he felt that life had spat in his face.

★ ★ ★

Through the little notebook I travelled a road that passed from flowering countryside to savage expanses full of pus, acid, and blood, black bile, pools of fire. As the days flew by, not only the landscape but Lysia Verhareine was changing, though the rest of us never saw any signs. Inside this beautiful girl, so sweet and delicate, was growing a creature who screamed in silence and tore at her own heart. A being in free fall who never stopped falling.

Sometimes her fiancé himself came to bear the brunt of her anguish, as she reproached him for his silence and the infrequency of his letters, doubting his love. But the following day she would never fail to offer him profuse apologies and caresses as tender as the first. It seems neither tack, however, moved him to write more often.

I can never know which camp he was in, this Bastien Francoeur: whether he was with the bastards or on the side of the just. I'll never know what sparkle may have been visible in his eye as he held one of Lysia's letters, when he opened and read it, if indeed he did. I'll never know if he kept those outpourings of hers with him in the trench, a suit of armour made of paper and of love, when the attack was about to start and his whole life whirled by him once more like a leering lurid carousel. For all I can know, he skimmed them wearily, perhaps with a dark suppressed laugh, before he crumpled them up and chucked them into a mud puddle.

The last letter, a short one filling the last page of the notebook, was dated 3 August, 1915. In it she still professes her love, in simple words; she speaks of the summer too, of the vast and beautiful days that are filled with nothing when one is waiting and alone. I'm abridging a bit, but not much. I could copy it out verbatim, but I don't want to. It's already enough that Destinat and I laid our eyes on the notebook, as though gazing through a window at someone undressing. There's no call for others to see this last letter. Let it remain sacred, her farewell to the world, her final words — even if the young teacher wrote them scarcely dreaming they would be her last.

Following this letter, there's nothing more. Nothing but blankness, pages and pages unmarked. The blankness of death.

'Death inscribed'.

26

When I say there's nothing more, I'm lying.
I'm lying twice over, in fact.

In the first place there's a letter, though not
from Lysia. A little sheet, slipped into the
notebook after her final words, signed by a
certain Captain Brandieu, on 27 July, 1915. It
must have arrived at the château on August 4.
That much is clear.

Mademoiselle,
It is with great sadness that I bring you
this news: ten days ago, during an assault
on the enemy lines, Corporal Bastien
Francoeur was struck in the head by a
sniper's bullet. Aided by his comrades,
he was brought back to our trench,
where a medic could do no more than
bind his wound. Corporal Francoeur
died in the minutes that followed without
regaining consciousness.

I hope it will be of comfort to know
that he died a soldier's death for his
country. In the months he was under my
command, he conducted himself with an
unwavering stout heart, always first to

volunteer for the most dangerous missions. He was loved by his men and esteemed by his superiors.

Please forgive my ignorance of the nature of your relationship with Corporal Francoeur, Mademoiselle, but as several of your letters have arrived since his death, I thought it well to inform you of his tragic end, in case word had not yet reached you from his family, who are some distance from you.

Rest assured, Mademoiselle, that I share in your grief and offer my sincerest condolences.

Captain Charles-Louis Brandieu

It's strange, the varied instruments of death. You imagine a knife, a bullet, a shell, but those aren't the only ones. A little letter can be as lethal; a mere letter, full of fine sentiments and compassion, can kill as surely as any weapon.

Lysia Verhareine received this letter. I don't know whether she cried out, wept, screamed, or fell silent. I'll never know. All I can say is that within a few hours the prosecutor and I were in her room, standing over her body, looking at each other without understanding. At least I didn't understand. He already knew, or soon would, upon finding the red morocco notebook.

Why had he taken it? To preserve the memory of their dinner, so he could continue to live with the miracle of her smiles and her words? Something like that, I suppose.

The soldier, the beloved, was dead. For him she had abandoned everything, for him she had climbed to the crest each Sunday, for him she had taken up her pen every day. It was for him that her heart beat. And this beloved soldier, had he seen any face before him when the bullet shattered his skull? Lyse? Another woman? No one? A mystery, and quite beside the point.

★   ★   ★

I've often imagined Destinat poring over the notebook, coming to the testaments of love that must have pained him, seeing himself called Sadness and mocked — though with a gentle, affectionate mockery. He didn't get his right between the eyes, as I did!

Yes, reading again and again, just as you might continually turn over an hourglass, to pass the time watching the sand flow, nothing more.

I said a while ago that I was lying twice over. Besides the letter slipped into the notebook, there were also three photographs.

They were pasted side by side on the final page. And this little scene of frozen cinema had been composed by none other than Destinat.

In the first picture you could recognise the model who'd posed for the painter of the large portrait in the entrance hall: Clélis de Vincey might have been seventeen then. Here she was in a meadow dotted with umbellifers, the ones we call meadow-sweet. A girl laughing. She wore country clothes, and the simplicity only accentuated her elegance. A wide-brimmed hat cast a dark shadow across half her face but could not obscure her dazzled grace, her eyes in the light, her smile, the sun glow of her hand as she held down the brim lofted by the wind. She was the sweetness of the meadow.

The second photograph had been rough-cut from a larger, broader one, and in that oddly elongated slice a happy little girl looked straight out. In this way Destinat's scissors had isolated Morning Glory from the photograph Bourrache had given him. 'Just like the Blessed Virgin,' her father had told me, and he was right. The little girl's face radiated something religious, a beauty without artifice, a goodness, a simple splendour.

In the third photograph, Lysia Verhareine was leaning against a tree, her hands flat against the bark, her chin raised a bit, her mouth half open. She seemed to be waiting for a kiss from the one holding the camera. She was just as I had known her. It was only her expression that had changed. She had never offered any of us that smile. It was the unmistakable smile of desire, of mad love, and it was very disturbing to see her this way, because with that her mask had dropped; you understood her true nature and what she was capable of doing for the man she loved — or to herself.

Still, the strangest effect of all this — and it wasn't the result of my having drunk a fair amount — was the impression of gazing at three portraits of the same face, the same face at various ages, in different moments of history, even.

Morning Glory, Clélis, and Lysia were like three incarnations of the same soul, a soul that had lent to the bodies it had worn an identical smile, a sweetness, and a fire without equal. The same beauty, returning again and again, born and destroyed, reappearing and gone. Seeing them side by side like this made your head swim. You went from one to the next, only to see the same. There was something pure and demonic in all that, inspiring a mixture of serenity and dread. Before so much constancy, you could almost believe that beauty persists, no matter what and in spite of time, and that what was will return.

I thought of Clémence, and at once it seemed to me I could have added a fourth photograph. And with that it seemed I was taking leave of my senses. I closed the notebook. I had too great an ache, too many thoughts, too many storms in my head. And all that on account of three little photographs, placed in a row by a lonely old man, well acquainted with boredom.

It occurred to me to burn everything.

I didn't do it. Professional habit. You don't destroy evidence. But evidence of what? Of our hopeless incapacity to see the living as they are? None of us had ever said, 'How about that? Bourrache's little girl is the spitting image of Lysia Verhareine. Two peas in a pod!' Barbe had never said, 'That little teacher — it's eerie how much she looks like the late Madame Destinat!'

But maybe only death could reveal that. Maybe it was only the prosecutor and I who could see it. Maybe the two of us were alike in madness as in other things.

When I think of those two long hands of Destinat, well-manicured and delicate, covered with speckles of age and taut with tendons; when I see them early on a winter's evening, squeezing the fragile, slender neck of Morning Glory, as the child's smile ebbs from her face and a big question fills her eyes — when I imagine this scene that took place, or didn't take place, I tell myself that Destinat wasn't strangling a little girl but a memory, a suffering. That suddenly in his hands, under his fingers, it was the ghosts of Clélis and Lysia Verhareine whose necks he was trying to wring so he could be rid of them forever; so he would no longer hear or see them, feel their approach at night and extend his hand to reach them; so he would love them in vain no more.

But it's not so easy to kill the dead. To make them go away. How many times have I tried it myself. Everything would be so much simpler if it were otherwise.

And so other faces would have passed into the face of the child, this little girl whose path he'd crossed by chance, at the end of a snowy, frosty day, as night began to gather and with it all those tormenting shades. Suddenly love and crime would have become confused, as though in that moment you could kill only what you loved, and that alone.

I lived for a long time with this idea of Destinat as murderer by mistake — out of illusion, hope, memory, dread. I found it beautiful. Not that it altered the fact of murder, but this way it seemed sublime, high above the sordid facts. Both criminal and victim made martyrs: That's unusual.

And then one day a letter reached me. We know when letters are sent. There's no telling why they never arrive, why they take so long. Could it be that the young corporal also wrote every day to Lysia Verhareine? Might his letters be in transit somewhere still, wandering through byways, labyrinths of human conveyance, even with the sender and the addressed long dead?

The letter I'm speaking of now had been mailed from Rennes on 23 March, 1919. It had taken six years to get here. Six years just to cross France.

It had been addressed to me by a colleague. He didn't know me, and I didn't know him. He must have sent the same letter to all of us who had drowsed in towns near the front during the war.

Alfred Vignot — that was his name — wanted to track down a fellow he'd lost sight of since 1916. We at the station often received similar requests, from city halls, from families, from other policemen. The war had been a big broth stirring with hundreds of thousands of men. Some were dead, others had survived. Some had gone back home;

others tried to start a new life, unseen and unknown. The great butchery had not only chopped up bodies and minds, it had also allowed a small number to let themselves be reported missing, so they might try their luck far from their native region, to have another spin of the wheel, so to speak. You had to be very clever to prove they were alive, especially since it had become so easy to change names and acquire documents. After all, there were about a million and a half who'd never need their names and documents again: plenty to choose from! And so, just like that, a lot of bastards blossomed all over again, popping up smelling of roses, far from the places that had seen them down in the dung pile.

Vignot's missing person had a death to answer for, a dead girl to be exact. He had tortured her meticulously — the details were given in the letter — before strangling and raping her. The crime had been committed in May of 1916, and it had taken Vignot three years to complete his inquiry, gather the evidence, be sure of his facts. The victim's name was Blanche Fen'vech. She was ten years old. They had found her near a footpath, left in a ravine, less than a kilometre from the village of Plouzagen. That's where she lived. She had set out as every evening to look for four wretched cows in a meadow. I didn't have to read it through to guess who Vignot was after. Soon as I had opened the envelope, it was as if someone was reading over my shoulder, hovering inside my head.

His man was named Le Floc, Yann Le Floc. He would have been nineteen at the time of the murder. He was my little Breton.

★ ★ ★

I never answered Vignot. To each his own shit! No doubt he was right about Le Floc, but that didn't change a thing. The little girls were dead, the one in Brittany and the one here in our town. The kid was dead too, executed by firing squad, by the book. And deep down I couldn't dismiss the idea that Vignot might have been mistaken or that maybe he had reasons of his own for framing the boy, just as those scumbags Mierck and Matziev had had theirs. Who knows?

Strangely enough, I was now well accustomed to living with mystery, with doubt, dimness, hesitation — long deprived of answers and certainties. Replying to Vignot would have swept all that away; with one fell swoop there would have been clarity, turning Destinat snow-white, plunging the little Breton into blackness. Too simple. One of the two had killed, certainly, but the other could have done it just as well, and there is no essential difference between the intention and the crime.

I took Vignot's letter and lit the bowl of my pipe with it. Bah! Smoke! Cloud! Ashes! Nothingness! Keep on trying to find my man, so I won't be the only one on this case! Maybe it was spite, in fact. A way of believing I wasn't the only one digging in the dirt with his nails, trying to unearth the dead and make them talk. Even in the void, we need to know that there are other men like us.

27

There you are: we've reached the end. The story's end and mine. The graves, like the mouths, have been stopped up a long time now, and the dead are no more than names on stones, half worn away: Morning Glory, Lysia, Destinat, Solemn, Barbe, Adélaïde Siffert, the little Breton and the typographer, Mierck, Gachentard, Bourrache's wife, Hippolyte Lucy, Mazerulles, Clémence. Often I imagine them — all of them, the men, the women, the little girl — in the cold earth and its packed darkness. I know that their eye sockets are long since empty, the flesh withered from their interlaced fingers.

If somebody wanted to know what I've been up to all these years, all the time that's brought me to this point, I wouldn't know for sure how to answer. I can't say I saw the years pass, though all of them have seemed very long to me. I've kept a flame going and interrogated the darkness, without ever getting more than partial answers, tight-lipped and piecemeal.

But it's been a living, this dialogue with the dead. Enough to keep me going, while waiting for the end. I've spoken to Clémence. I've recalled the others. Scarcely a day goes by when I don't summon them before me to pore over their gestures and words yet again, wondering whether I understood them correctly the last time.

Just when I believe at last I've caught a glimmer of the truth, right away something else comes along and blows out the light, swirling the ashes around my eyes. And everything has to be revisited.

But maybe that's the key to my having endured: this dialogue in a single voice, always the same, always mine, and the opaqueness of this crime that has no culprit, perhaps, except the opaqueness of our very lives. Life is extremely odd. Do we ever know why we've come into the world and why we've stayed here? No doubt delving into the Case as I've done was a way of evading the real question, the one we all refuse to pose with our lips and in our minds, in our souls — which indeed are neither white nor black but 'nice and grey', just as Joséphine had told me without a doubt in her mind.

I've told you everything, I believe. Everything about what I thought I was — or almost. There's only one thing still to say, the most difficult perhaps, something I've never even murmured. And so for that let me take another drink, to screw up the courage, to say it to you, Clémence, since it's for you alone that I speak and write, as from the beginning, now and always.

I couldn't bear to give him a name or even look at him, really. I didn't kiss him as a father should have done.

When the tall nun in a wimple, dry as autumn fruit left in the oven too long, brought him to me a week after your death, she said, 'This is your child. He has only you now.' She did no more to install him here than to put the white bundle in my arms before being on her way. The child was asleep. He felt very warm and smelled sweetly of milk. His face peeked out of cloth that swaddled him like a baby Jesus in a creche, and his cheeks were so chubby that his mouth was lost in their fullness. I looked for your face in his, imagining a keepsake you might have sent me from the afterlife. But he didn't look like anything — nothing like you, anyway. He looked like all other newborns, those who've just seen the light of day after a long cosy night spent in a place we all forget. Yes, he was one of them: an innocent, as they say. The future of the world. A human baby. The perpetuation of the race. But for my part, I could see in him only the one who'd taken your life, a little murderer without conscience or remorse; and I could see I would have to live with him though you weren't here any longer, though he'd killed you to make his way to me, though he'd used his elbows and all the rest to get here and face me alone. And while I'd never see your face again or kiss your skin, he would grow every day, soon cutting teeth to go on devouring, hands to grab things and eyes to see them; and then, later, he'd have words, words to tell his great lie to whoever cared to listen: that he had never known you, that you had died giving birth, when in fact he killed you in order to live.

I didn't think it over very long. It just happened. I picked up a big pillow and made his face disappear. I waited there, a long time. He didn't move. To use the terms of those who judge us here on earth, there was no premeditation; it was all I could do, and so I did it. I took the pillow away and I cried, thinking not of him but of you.

I went to look for Hippolyte Lucy, to tell the doctor the baby wasn't breathing. He came with me in haste. He entered the room. The baby was on the bed, still with that face of an innocent sleeper, peaceful and monstrous.

The doctor undressed him. He bent down to hold his cheek near the closed mouth. He listened to the heart; it was no longer beating. He said nothing. He shut his bag and he turned to me.

We faced each other, a long time. He knew. I knew he did, but he said nothing. He left me alone with the little body.

I had him buried next to you. Ostrane said that newborns vanish into the ground like a perfume in the wind, before you've even had the chance to notice it. He meant no harm. The thought seemed to fill him with wonder.

I didn't inscribe his name on the gravestone.

The worst I must confess is that even today I feel no remorse. I'd do it again with no more qualms than when I did it then, which is to say none. I'm not proud of it. I'm not ashamed of it either. It wasn't pain that drove me to it. It was emptiness. Not the fear of it but the desire for it. The emptiness where I've remained, and where I wanted to remain alone. He would've had no luck, an unhappy little boy growing up with a father for whom life was no more than a void filled with a single question — a great bottomless hole, along whose rim I'd be forever picking my way, round and round, talking to you, and clinging to my words like the walls of a deep well.

Yesterday I went and loafed around the

Pont des Voleurs. Do you remember? How old could we have been, not yet twenty? You were wearing a red dress. My stomach clenched up. We were on the bridge, looking down at the river. This current, you told me — look how far it goes, how beautiful it is, there among the water lilies, the algae with the long hair, the banks of clay. I didn't dare put my arm around your waist. The knot in my gut was so unbearable I could hardly breathe. Your eyes gazed off into the distance. Mine were looking at the nape of your neck. I smelled your perfume of heliotrope and the fragrance of the river, the freshness of trodden grass. Then, without my expecting it, you turned to me with a smile and gave me a kiss. It was the first time. And the water flowed under the bridge. The world shone as on some beautiful Sunday, and time meant nothing.

Yesterday I lingered on the Pont des Voleurs a long while. The river is the same. Those big water lilies, the algae with long hair, those clay banks are still there. The scent of the grass. A child came up to me, a boy with light-coloured eyes. 'Looking at the fish?' he asked. 'There's a lot, but you never see them,' he added, a little disappointed. I made no reply. There are so many things you never see. He leaned on his elbows beside me, and we stayed that way quite a while, amid the music of the frogs and the eddies, he and I. When I left, the boy followed me for a bit; then he disappeared.

Today it's all done. I've spent my time, and the emptiness no longer scares me. Maybe you think I'm a bastard like the rest, no better than the others. You'd be right, of course. Forgive me for everything I've done and, even more, for everything I haven't done.

I hope you'll be able to judge for yourself, face-to-face. I suddenly hope that God does exist, and along with him the whole kit and caboodle, all the nonsense they crammed into our heads when we were little. If it's so, you'll have a hard time recognising me. You left behind a young man, and I return to you an old one, almost old, grizzled and scarred anyway. You haven't changed, I know. The dead never do.

A while ago, I took down Gachentard's rifle. I took it apart, oiled it, cleaned and polished it. I put it back together, loaded it, and set it here beside me at the window. Hard to imagine the girl didn't notice its beauty. Outside, the weather is mild and bright. Today's a Monday. It's morning. A fine time for a story to end.

We do hope that you have enjoyed reading this large print book.

Did you know that all of our titles are available for purchase?

We publish a wide range of high quality large print books including:
Romances, Mysteries, Classics
General Fiction
Non Fiction and Westerns

Special interest titles available in large print are:
The Little Oxford Dictionary
Music Book
Song Book
Hymn Book
Service Book

Also available from us courtesy of Oxford University Press:
Young Readers' Dictionary
(large print edition)
Young Readers' Thesaurus
(large print edition)

For further information or a free brochure, please contact us at:
Ulverscroft Large Print Books Ltd.,
The Green, Bradgate Road, Anstey,
Leicester, LE7 7FU, England.
Tel: (00 44) 0116 236 4325
Fax: (00 44) 0116 234 0205

Other titles published by Ulverscroft:

MONSIEUR LINH AND HIS CHILD

Philippe Claudel

Traumatized by memories of his war-ravaged country, his son and daughter-in-law dead, Monsieur Linh travels to a foreign land to bring the child in his arms to safety. To begin with, he is too afraid to leave the refugee centre — but the first time he braves the freezing cold to walk the streets of this strange, fast-moving town, he encounters Monsieur Bark, a widower whose dignified sorrow mirrors his own. Though they have no shared language, an instinctive friendship is forged between them . . .